PRAISE FOR
SISTER GOLDEN CALF

"I was blown away by *Sister Golden Calf*, a wise and brutally intimate exploration of sisterhood and grief and the bonds that tie us to each other. Magical and hypnotic, poetic and fierce, every line contains a universe, and nothing is spared. Gloria and Kit will stay with me for a long time. Colleen Burner is an unmistakable talent."

—Chelsea Bieker, author of *Godshot* and *Heartbroke*

"In Colleen Burner's stunning debut novella, *Sister Golden Calf*, a pair of sisters roam the New Mexico deserts with their beloved mother's cremains, their only plan: 'burying bits of her ash and smudging her all over her home state.' These are young women sensitive to the faintest traces of grace and beauty in the world; Burner recreates the usual buddy-buddy road trip as an intensely female narrative of longing and landscape, both metaphysical and sensual, in a gorgeous prose that puts the ineffable into wise words and brings the invisible into illuminating view."

—Tara Ison, author of *At the Hour Between Dog and Wolf*

"'When a man steps onto the road, his journey begins. When a woman steps onto that same road, hers ends,' said Vanessa Veselka, in her examination of the absence of female road narratives. Colleen Burner's *Sister Golden Calf* imagines an otherwise. How would a story move—at what speed, at what gait—and what shape would it take, what mood would it assume, if it followed, not Quixote or Kerouac, but two misfit sisters on the road? Upon the cracked highways of New Mexico, yes, but also the road of grief, of what it means to drive into one's heartbreak and yet keep on living. *Sister Golden Calf* travels the mysteries of what can't be captured in language and invites us, the hitchhiking reader, with a warm hand and open door, along for the ride."

—David Naimon, host of *Between the Covers* podcast

"*Sister Golden Calf* is my favorite kind of novel: compact and meditative, delightfully strange, elegiac but awash in warm light and the promise of ineffable treasure in each sentence. Amid the variegated desert landscape and seductive kismet of the open road, the sisters face questions of longing and belonging, of how to care for each other and themselves, and of what artifacts to carry as they carry on. Colleen Burner has stolen my heart with this novel."

—Alexis Smith, author of *Marrow Island* and *Glaciers*

"In shiveringly beautiful prose, Colleen Burner maps a wild voyage into grief, love, and radical forms of kinship. Their novel unstitches the fixed seams of self and stranger, inviting us to touch the peculiar, precise commotions that link one creature to another. A truly extraordinary book."

—Leni Zumas, author of *Red Clocks*

SISTER

GOLDEN

CALF

SISTER

GOLDEN

CALF

COLLEEN BURNER

Published by Split/Lip Press
PO Box 27656
Ralston, NE 68127
www.splitlippress.com

ISBN: 978-1-952897-31-3

Cover and Book Design: David Wojciechowski
Cover Photograph: Ganapathy Kumar, Unsplash
Editing: Kate Finegan

To KM, for taking the trip.

When the planet tilted us into spring, Kit and I found ourselves pacing like dogs. Warm air stirred and split through the sky; the atmosphere inside the house became charged and stifling. Bonnie's jar had sat on the mantel for not quite a year next to jars of SWAN DREAM, LIVING WICK, PETRIFIED AIR, TEEMING PERIPHERY, her prized possessions handed down from each generation of matrilineal ephemerists, all labeled to identify what was unseen inside. Bonnie's jar needed no label. Kit and I had been looking at it, together—always together—ever since we brought it home, trying to untangle grief from the rest of life. One dawn, Kit looked me hard in the eye and said, "Wanna go for a ride?" The simplest solution: we both felt it, were likely to boil over if we didn't make a move, and quick. We spent the morning packing up jars and supplies, readying to trade the familiarity of the house for the familiarity of travel. We took a deep breath and stepped out the door.

PART I

I like to see us from the outside. Pressed under the blue sky, bright and deep, and over narrow blacktop, dry grasses, faraway fists of red rock: one 1993 Honda Accord LX. Automatic transmission, sunroof, AM/FM radio, muffler tied with a piece of wire, empty back seat and a full trunk. The body is Rosewood Brown, which is like a warm silver, and from a distance it looks like a mouse running under the rug of the New Mexico sky.

Kit and I swung out of Silver River I don't know how many days or weeks ago. She has that look on her face that's about the past, replaying what's already happened, trying to play out how things may go in the future. A mental chewing.

"Pretend the car is a horse," I say.

She looks at me. "Why?"

"We'll go faster. It'll feel more like a Western," I say as I jerk my arms up and down, holding onto the steering wheel like reins. "I used to pretend my bike was a horse," I tell her. "When I had a bike."

"I'm too seat-belted in to feel horseness, Gloria."

I tell her, "It'll feel more real when the road's rougher."

*

Headed north on US-491, the car ahead of us swerves and pitches a brown round thing up in the air. We hadn't seen it before it was flying. The car ahead rights itself and keeps driving. I steer the Honda to the shoulder. We each grab a jar from the trunk. We find what the car hit because it's bigger than the other brown rocks by the road and shuddering breath in and out. An armadillo. Kit holds her jar to its snout and I put mine over its tail and the armadillo curls into its tight ball. The tail makes a clink when it taps against the mouth of my jar. I'll label it TAIL NOTE.

Kit doesn't feel like anything's gone from snout to jar, not even a last breath. It seems more like the creature's soul stayed coiled up inside it. One of its feet is crushed and blood runs from a gash in its armored skin, tracing through the ripples and grooves. Its ancient protection is no match for brazen, combustion-engined human progress. We bury it, but only halfway in case some live thing comes looking to scavenge a meal. The arc of its back bumps out of the dirt like it burrowed itself.

*

INVENTORY: the trunk rattles with boxes of jars to sell and trade. Jars that held peanut butter and jelly, mayonnaise, baby food, pickles, spices, olives, salsa, as well as the long-favored Ball jars, all cleansed of their food ghosts, rid of their former labels, the paper and glue still deep under a few of our fingernails.

The jars now contain such things as: SOMEONE ELSE'S DREAMS, NIGHTMARES, BELL CHIMES, A LAST BREATH, LAST WORDS, THE BIG PLUNGE, LATE AFTERNOON DREAM, DEAD LIGHT, NIGHT GREASE, STRATOSPHERE, VOID, COLD STREAMS OF LOGIC, HOLES, SMOOTH, CLOUD FEELING, POINT OF AIM, and SOULS OF WILD ANIMALS, SOULS OF DOMESTICATED ANIMALS, SOUL OF A WILD PERSON (a family heirloom).

Sometimes sold on the side of the road, like corn or tomatoes, sometimes at gas stations, to anyone who recognizes that the jars aren't empty—that they're full of invisible things for feeling and knowing. It's the opposite of peddling snake oil, Bonnie would say. Still, I think of what to say that might help convince: "Yes, it's invisible, but it really is there. Like gravity, or helium."

Near the intersection of I-40 and 371, our sign is up, our bright green blanket hanging out of our open trunk and flapping in the wind. Our sign, carefully serifed script, black on white: MOST EVERYTHING THAT EXISTS, IN A JAR. A woman on an old Triumph Tiger pulls over, pulls off her helmet to see our stock. She twists inside her leathers and her back cracks loudly.

Kit hovers her hand over our spread, holds up a twelve-ounce jar. "This," she says, "is a coyote soul."

"Looks pretty small for a coyote, don't you think?"

"Coyotes are a relatively small animal. A human soul isn't much bigger, actually."

I add: "Wild things tend to be smaller. Take, for instance, the organically-grown vegetable."

She turns her face away and squints. "I don't know if I want to haul around some malnourished coyote. I'm used to being alone."

"You've been to old places with lower ceilings, shorter doorways, haven't you? Everyone was smaller compared to nowadays, back when we grew different," I say, trying.

Kit reaches the jar toward the woman. "I felt it call to you," she says. "Try holding it."

The woman takes off a glove, wraps her hand around the jar. Warm skin on warm glass. The lid reflects a patch of light onto her face, illuminates small lines of scars around her mouth. She smiles at the jar.

"You feel that?" Kit says softly. She's better at this part, making it an invitation rather than a challenge.

"Yeah, kind of like…four new legs running in my pulse," the woman says. She looks down the road. "How much?"

"Enough to put a couple gallons in our Honda."

Kit and the woman make the exchange, shake hands.

She gently packs the jar into a saddle bag, climbs back onto the bike, says, "What if I open it?"

"A howl, an escape."

The Tiger tears down the road and that's our only trade that afternoon.

What we collect is either animal or atmosphere. The animal tends to be more urgent, as they're typically in transit from alive to dead. Some things are shy, obscured, and capturing them feels sublime but quick and ecliptic. It's something that's almost on you like static electricity, or you think you can barely see it like a floater in your eye—present and right in front of you, fleeting and skittish the more you try to look at it—or rolling over you, a churning at your feet like a private fog. Some are easy as odors and fill the jar on their own. Other soul-based specters have a strong clarity, like recognizing the ghost of yourself while you're still alive, watching it make circles around you in another body. A doubled feeling. But the more subtle ethers—sometimes it doesn't occur to you what it is until the lid's screwed tight. I don't mean this as an easy thing: it's not like picking berries from a bush. It's a focused stillness, a meditating without losing location, a sensing with your heart-gut. Dowsing without moving, or maybe you're what's being dowsed for.

I think I was about four the first time—I know I was small enough to get engulfed in Bonnie's lap, and four was her favorite number. I remember my hands not wrapping all the way around the empty jar (which previously held cherry pie filling), and her hands clasping over mine from behind while I sat against her. I remember the light being that syrupy golden kind, the kind that when you stand in it makes you feel preserved in amber, or ambrosia, filtering through piñon trees, illuminating flittering insects and bits of flora in the air. This light on her hands made them robust and opaque, erasing the revelation of veins under thin skin, the veins that roped over tendons or bones and made me think FRAGILE, FRAGILE.

In this fiery light we held the jar, together, on the ground. A sort of posture lesson: *Don't sag the elbows too much or you won't be alert; don't rest your jar against anything; try to blend in with the air around you.* And then we waited.

What I expected: a shimmering like suspended dust in sunlight or what's on your hands after holding fool's gold; something like lightning to jolt into the jar; something clearly there and then immediately not there, like a puff of smoke. A visible magic.

We waited. The light shifted. Then the feeling of a great density gently easing into the jar, just for a second, and then Bonnie whispered, "Now." I spun the lid on and held the jar up in my small hands, made a label with crooked lettering: YOUNG SAP.

Over time I learned that, for me, the feeling isn't always so clear, learned that there is a sense deeper than proprioception to tune into. As a kid, I used to walk around the house with my eyes closed, my hands reaching out for walls and corners to guide me. Now my hands are constantly reaching out. There's something secretive inside that recognizes what is being caught, and because of this elusiveness, it can be hard to be sure of. I capture these invisible things carefully, without trickery. Although more and more, I'm not sure that's possible. Can an invisible be caught with honesty? Does it want to be captured and jarred? Does it want at all? It's not as if the jars, once filled, rattle and shake or show obvious signs of protest. I'm not sure how much this is like taming a feral animal, keeping them indoors, hoping they'll be assuaged by having a safe place to sleep. Hoping they'll understand containment is just something to get used to.

I've been thinking hard on it lately; it's different without the standard of Bonnie to hold ourselves to, and it's our trade—it's keeping us on the road and able to *be*, which is good, but something is tugging on my inner sleeve. How much longer can we go? I wonder if Kit has an end in mind but it seems too late or too early to ask.

*

INVENTORY: a two-quart Mason jar with a shiny gold lid, no label, our biggest. Now half-full of cremains, dispersed bit by bit as we go. The gray grit of Bonnie clings to its smooth walls like a fact, the human equivalent of a ship in a bottle. Our Matriarch, full of mirth. She waitressed right up to the moment of her death at 70, carrying a tray of strawberry milkshakes on her shoulder, her head held high and hair done up—*like a wedding cake*, I used to tell her—tiers of hair, blue-rinsed and proud, when she slipped on a cherry pit. When Kit told me, I pictured Bonnie's beautiful head cake cracked in the spill, saw it all creamy pink in red against the black and white of her uniform and the tile. I imagined the sharp sound it made and that it could still be echoing. Kit saw it happen and insisted there was no blood, but she didn't touch dairy or red fruits for a few months after.

Bonnie's jar stays in the front seat. I'm sitting on the ground on one of our blankets, jars of INTERSTELLAR, TINY STAMPEDE, and EROS/ION set out in front of me. Kit's spreading a handful of Bonnie by a yucca. I'm aware that it's a nice moment; I'm suspended in it, calm. No cars have gone by for a few hours but I'm not worried. Enjoying just the three of us, here.

*

It's one of those weeks, I guess, when you don't take off your shoes, or don't remember taking them off. When you scrub at your face only to find it's just dirty with sun tan. I'm grateful my hair withstands less washing, even though this is a vain thing to be grateful for. I don't want to be concerned with *looking bad.* Looking at myself in the long mirror at a rest-stop bathroom, I don't know if I look bad or good, I don't know my reference point.

I sit in a stall and hear a few car doors slam, then a few other stall doors bang shut and latch on either side of me. A brief silence, then one by one our pelvic muscles relax. I pay attention to our different pitches and rhythms reverberating against water and toilet bowls. A piss choir. I wonder if something like this could be practiced and performed, imagine this particular bathroom giving way to a concert hall, an amphitheater, the performers hidden by stalls. I keep imagining this after my own stream gives up, after I'm the only woman in the bathroom.

*

Saying grace: big burrito swimming in sauce and beans, bountiful barge of food, size of a fanny pack, little sleeping-bean-bag, most beautiful envelope of sustenance, guarantee of belly warmth satisfaction. Oh, baby. In our eyes, you are smothered in gold. *Amen.*

*

Kit believes she feels the jar get heavier each time something goes inside it. I wouldn't be surprised if Kit had a stronger connection to forces of nature, but I don't know if she's making it up or if I've been doing it wrong. Maybe it's different for every person. Bonnie taught each of us how to do it separately, and she once said I was like a tiger trap while Kit was a pounce in slow motion. It doesn't feel right to question if one of us is doing it "wrong," but we're sisters. Comparison finds ways to creep in.

*

Feeling grimy in a lot of sweat and dirt while trying to sleep tonight. The old awful restlessness of feeling like I can't breathe in enough, like my lungs are sails not quite catching wind. Discomfort from all this shifting around, trying to fill the space of loss, rears up again. Overwhelms. An interior, choking homesickness. An animal trapped inside me, clawing at the walls. I try to explain it to Kit: "A feeling of *I'm not really here* as well as *I'm here too much*."

"Should we try to outrun it?" Kit asks.

We drive a few miles before seeing the sign for a motel boasting a pool. We take the exit, turn into the parking lot, headlights off, drive up to the iron fence. Waves of moonlight swaying. We leave the car doors unlocked. Shuffle out of some clothes, climb on the trashcan and over the fence, clattering of folding chairs, and in we jump—cool blue rush and immersion like the whole body drinking, like a sponge, coming up through darkness and the brain reorienting.

Back above water I gasp in and my sails fill. I'm a Ball of Jericho that's been waiting, waiting, waiting in the desert. I've been dry and dusty and closed for so long. A return to water, disruptive in the best way.

We don't say anything yet. We float for a time.

"You still feel trapped in there?"

"Not so much. I know it'll be back, but something about immersion…"

"You won't always have a pool to break into, you know."

"I know."

"So then what?"

"I know you love to problem solve," *and problem make, in your own way*, I think.

I move my hands and feet just enough to spin me a little as I float, stars and streetlights melting together over me. When I start thinking I could fall asleep we climb out, soggy and dripping back over the fence and shake like dogs. All of the quenched feeling holds inside me.

INVENTORY: a matchbook-sized sewing kit. Figure-eights of wound thread in black, brown, blue, pink. A small brown button. Three needles, three pins. My favorite travel accessory.

I wiggle a pin out of its slot. Sitting on the warm sidewalk at a rest stop, my head, neck, shoulders are resting in Kit's lap, arched to expose the small itchy bump on the underside of my chin.

I say, "This must be my fluke hair. Do you ever get those? Remember Bonnie had one on her shoulder and it was so long the end of it poked out of her shirt sleeve?"

"Stop talking or I can't see it."

"Okay." I shut my mouth.

"I meant a short-sleeved shirt sleeve," I say.

Putting her left index finger and thumb on either side of the in-grown hair, she pulls my skin taut. "There it is," she says, "tiny line coiled just below the surface." She holds the pin flush with the skin and pokes. I try not to flinch. I study Kit's face above mine, years of concentration already etching in lines, echoes of attention and focus, determination. I wonder if she has ever studied me so intently before. I feel her use the tip of the pin like a crowbar against the hair, but it's rooted tight. I picture the skin flushing red, a minute drop of blood. I wonder if Kit can also hear the faint snapping of the point against the hair. Finally something breaks free; the end of the hair is loosened and uncoils from the skin.

"Got it."

"Oh, thank god." I open my eyes. "How long is it?"

She teases its length out. "Almost an inch, I'd say. Fluke hair indeed. You want it plucked?"

I smile and sit up, say, "I'll let it flap in the breeze a little."

*

A small museum dedicated to Billy the Kid, packed with artifacts from the earlier half of the twentieth century. Between two yellow blossoming cacti outside, we leave some ashes. Her favorite blooms. Inside, rooms of antique guns, tools, and saddles give way to roomfuls of buggies, cameras, typewriters, and more guns and more tools; a museum of brown things made of leather and rust. Walking into the room of equine equipment, I fall in love. A sign taped to the glass case: *SIAMESE HEREFORD CALF calf has 2 bodies and 8 legs Two legs are on top and six on the bottom This calf was born on the Dickenson Ranch in 1942. Purchased and put on display in 1958*. It doesn't say when the calf died. Animal magnetism unto me. The impossible object, confoundedly made to be at home in the world—the natural world that's always trying new ways of surviving, not this indoor world of industrial artifact.

"Hello, spectacular creature," I say, crouching down to see her face. One eye stares over my shoulder.

The calf looks like something that might've grown out of the ground. All lump and leg. Mangy and eaten away at, absolutely dead and still aging. Two bodies fighting over a single head at one end, legs in a tangle at the other, flanked by two tails. Splendor of her fearful symmetry.

"How did you ever stand up or walk on your own? How long was your life? And how on earth were you birthed?"

"Oh, how you love an abnormality," Kit says behind me. (In the past: a wingless chick precious pet, fascination with news stories of frogs altered by chemical dumps, conjoined faces of daisies.)

An outlaw by nature, I think. Didn't even have to shoot anybody. "You are perfect," I tell the calf. "You are peculiar and beautiful and tremendous."

I stare and try to memorize all of her deteriorating details—whorls of fine tawny hairs, the angles of the joints in the sprawling legs, the grain of the hooves, it all seems like a holy text that's written only within her body—until Kit's made her way through the rest of the museum and comes back to drag me away. She's burned into my vision: the silhouette floats and glows wherever I look.

*

At Dos Caimanes, we drink free refills of hot black coffee, split a burrito platter (red side Kit's, green side mine). The sky is dark through the diner window, big curtains of clouds shutting down the sunset to a thin strip of fluorescent pink like the leg of a supine flamingo. Our secretly unshod feet pile on each other under the table. I lean back against the booth seat, feel my body gently swayed by my heartbeat. I'm thinking about the idea of outlaw, whether murder is necessary, if thievery is required. I wonder what kind of life the calf may have lived, what law of nature she defied. On a napkin, Kit makes the tally of jars to dollars to gas to miles, studying the map in her mind.

*

A night spent in the Honda, mountains edging the horizon outside every window. Knock-off Native woven blankets, all acrylic, no wool. The constant forward motion of the day's driving thrums through our muscles, a phantom throttling down the road. My foot thinks it steps on the gas and the highways go swirling around our heads. We roll and dream and roll and dream.

Sometimes I look at the invisible things in our jars and just think *all this is different parts of the universe here in one place* and then I remember that all the parts of the universe are always here anyways because it's all swimming and *here* is far as much as it is near. I think if any of the invisible things were visible they might look like the mirage that rises off the street, rippling and quaking.

We stop for gas in the early afternoon and while Kit pumps, I go in the store part and buy peanut butter and jelly and a loaf of bread. The jelly is in a glass jar we can use later. The girl at the counter is maybe sixteen. I pay in exact change and notice her duckish lips she hasn't grown into and maybe never will. Her name tag says KIMBERLEY. All ten of her fingers drum the countertop, chipped green polish at the bouncing fingertips. They're moving fast, as if she's not quite in control.

I pause, feeling the squish of soft bread under one hand, the hard, flat jar lids under the other. "Hey," I say, feeling bold, thinking maybe I can distract her from whatever's got her jittery, "do you think you have to see things to really believe them?"

Her eyes snap onto mine like she'd been waiting for someone to ask and she says, "Yes, I think so. But I don't think everyone can see things the same."

"Oh?"

"Well, these angels? Two of them. They've been fighting at the foot of my bed every night the past two years—doesn't matter what bed I'm in. Keeps me from getting good sleep but no one believes me that they're there. No one else has been able to see them. So, yeah, I do think you have to see things to believe, yes."

I don't know what I expected—ghosts, maybe, or mythical roadside attractions. "How can you tell they're angels?"

"They're kinda see-through, bluish and glowing. They look like what we put on top of our Christmas tree—like Marilyn Monroe with fluffy wings—they have wings different sizes and those gold hoops over their heads. They look nice but, god, they fight hard."

"What a nightmare."

"I mean, I wish it was just a nightmare. Then I could at least wake up from it. They don't make any noise, but they wrestle so rough the bed moves and thumps against the wall and wakes up the house. And no one believes me. It's like I can barely live without all that sleep."

I think of Kit and tell Kimberley I have something that might help. I gesture that I'll be right back and go out to the Honda. Kit's sitting on the trunk. I tell her what Kimberley told me and Kit slides off and opens our stock.

"What do you think?" I ask.

"Not an animal. Something…placid and galactic."

We pull different jars half out of their paper nestlings so we can read the labels.

"She needs something far away." I pick up a baby food jar near the back of the box: WHAT IS LEFT AFTER A STAR EXPLODES. "Maybe this."

Kit nods.

It's a little risky to choose from such a wide assortment for someone else, I think, rather than letting them feel what they need, be drawn to something. But there's also something to be said for the prescriptive element, of someone handing you what may be a solution, doing that work for you.

Back inside, I put the jar on the counter.

Kimberley looks anxious still, reads, "…*after a star*…How will this help? It sounds violent and they're already—"

"You just keep this with you," I say. "It's not like for inhaling or putting on your body, but it came from a place far away from Earth, a silent place, where there's this dark pocket of stillness, where whatever's capable of existing will be sleeping for a long time. In the way we measure time on Earth, I mean." She looks at me with her eyebrows raised so high I wonder if she thinks I'm an alien.

She lets out a big breath. "Okay. I mean, I'll try anything, I guess? Might as well. Is this what y'all do? Ride around delivering…whatever?" She holds the jar up, looks in, and her eyes wobble through the glass. "Looked like you have more in your trunk."

"We trade them. We've been traveling for a while."

"Mhmm." She punches some buttons on the cash register, the drawer rings open and she slams it shut. "Don't worry about the gas," she says. "People drive off all the time, so."

Then she empties the leave-a-penny-take-a-penny tray into her hand and empties her hand into mine, fingers still twitchy. "Boss calls these *karma pennies*," she says. "See how they treat you."

Outside, Kit's pulled the Honda around to the side of the store. I get in the passenger seat and pour the pennies into one of the cup holders.

"Small trade there," Kit says.

"Plus the gas. Don't fret, sister."

"Oh." Some muscle in her face unclenches, softens her. She hands me a sandwich. A wind must've blown through while she was making it because the inside is gritty between my teeth. But I like feeling land in my mouth.

*

A blessing: this small basket of sopapillas, sopapillows, little pouches with clouds of dough aroma tucked inside; we tear off corners with our teeth like hungrily opening love letters, vicious to get to the sweet honey writing on the inside like gold leaf. Ideally, I could crawl in and fall asleep. Surely that is what happens in a paradise. Mouthfuls of hallelujah.

*

Driving through Spaghetti Western-lookalike geography, except out here it's the real West, fake spaghetti. Thinking about movie cowboys, how I always wanted them to be the Robin Hood type but the only poor they ever seem to give to is themselves. I guess they don't promise they're going to be a hero. So American that way: shoot for loot, then ride off to some other territory. Staying nameless and shameless. I wonder if the calf ever had a name, something not marking her strange nature with disgust, a name that wouldn't make her seem like a sideshow. A name that embraced the goodness of her outsider-hood.

Sign after sign warning about hitchhikers and the state prison, about being near the border, all down this winding gray-stripe of highway that eventually leads us to the diner Bonnie had told us would be here. "Eat yer eggs an' have 'em too," she'd said.

It's a plain wood-sided house with a gravel front yard full of yucca and cacti and all kinds of shining, iridescent ornaments that spin gentle in the wind. We sit at a table on a back patio facing the bird yard. Red, black, white chickens, some more exotic and spangly-feathered than others. White geese, a few ducks, a flock of peacocks, and interloping sparrows and black birds. We marvel at their movements: so ungraceful, almost mechanical yet all their own, these animals preoccupied with their insatiable appetites and desire for authority and territory. We watch until the waitress slides our food before us on hot platters: generous tortillas stuffed with beans and peppers and slithers of onions, swimming in a pool of blood-red sauce. Kit's has a fried egg laying on top, the yolk sagging over the side.

"I just want to dip my whole face right in it," she says.

"Egg on your face, more ways than one." We smile at each other. "Very happy that this journey has brought us such bountiful plates," I say.

"Very happy that you are very happy. Hope we don't get sick of them."

I gesture toward outside with my fork and say, "Wonder which one of those girls your egg came from."

"Hopefully one who is living a fulfilling life, however brief it may be," she says.

"I wonder what kind of chicken and egg mishaps happen here."

"What, like mixing peacocks and chickens?"

"Like eggs with two yolks. Three yolks. Eggs with a little more chicken inside than intended."

"Glor'."

"What can go wrong in an egg, you know?" I grin.

"Thinking about that calf?"

"I'm just curious about the *odds*, is all. How frequently does one head get matched to two bodies? How often is it one body to two heads? And with that many limbs—the possibilities are endless!" I swipe the last corner of my burrito through the saucy carnage on my plate and stuff it in my mouth. "It's not just me, Kit," I say with my mouth full. "Someone else thought she was special enough to preserve."

Kit just laughs like she's heard this before.

The burritos are hot and the air outside is hot and soon our stomachs, already in the upper nineties, are full of more hot and the heat expands us, makes our hands and feet pink and heavy. The blood in my head is buzzing with spices. Tongue aflame.

After, we go and mingle with the birds. I don't tell Kit but I scatter a little Bonnie I had pocketed in their feed on the ground, which I think she'd enjoy. A pen of scraggly new ducks in the shade, a couple of the peacocks roost on top of it and their tails flow down the side like so much water. They caw and I wonder if it's aimed at us. It's the loudest thing I've heard in a while. Kit and I just look at them and wander around, reveling in being so close to creatures we'll never understand, who maybe don't understand each other. Food and territory: we have these concerns in common.

*

We stop for gas at a station that looks abandoned: tall sign rusted out, logo half-shattered, store windows full of dust and faded beer signs. But there's gas in the pumps and someone making change inside. Someone who looks like a middle-class mom (bright white sneakers and sensible, dry, bobbed hair) gets out of the minivan. *Do they even make minivans that aren't that color maroon anymore?* I wonder. We're on the other side of the pump, watching the gallons and cents tick up. I'm tired, hot, wind blowing the sweat cool on my back. The mom-woman plugs the nozzle into her gas tank and flinches when I say, "Excuse me, hi," but she turns around, doesn't lower her sunglasses. "You wanna buy a jarred soul?" I restrain myself from waggling my eyebrows at her. "Belonged to an elk, you look like the elk type—strong and kind of refined, you know?"

This is a lie I don't expect to tell. She looks more like the bowling shoe type. Kit managed to get something (UNSEEMLY LOVE) from a bowling shoe once. Never underestimate the powers retained by things that rapidly house various human-energy outlets, particularly ones that have "soles." I don't expect this woman to say anything back but she does:

"Does it have a shape—a physical form?"

Kit's glaring at me, eyes saying, *Do you have to be so casual with this really I am also tired come on.* I dig out the jar labeled ELK (COW) and show her. Our gas pumps thump at the same time. "You can't physically see it," I say, "but she's in this jar."

"Oh," the woman says, waving a hand at it, "I can't handle invisible things." She slides open the wide door of the van. No kids inside, just deep plastic tubs loaded with rocks. "I deal in minerals, stones, crystals—I need my energies in a physical form, you see. Something solid, something that won't escape."

"Huh."

"Would you like to buy one?" She asks in a cool, saleswoman voice.

"I—"

"Gloria. Tank's full," Kit says from the driver's seat.

Slightly crestfallen (crestwilted, crestslumped), I ask if I can just look at one. She leans into the van, finds something, holds her fist over my hand. A knuckle-sized piece of watery gray falls into my palm. "It's quartz," she says. "Smoky. Unclear." I roll it over my fingers, hear Kit buckle up.

"This isn't right for you, either," the woman says, voice low.

I know she knows. I say thank you, put the quartz back in her hand, and she holds my fingers for a second. "Good luck," I say.

"Same to you."

We do our best driving at dawn, when the light changes from blue to gold, and the landscape's events get revealed like a blanket pulling back. Rock formations and humps of bushes transform back from the sleeping things they become in the dark. Our little silvery Honda heralding the light, waking up the desert as we chase forward, trying to cover a distance before the sun does. The afternoon light is diamond-hard; the road is a long mercurial tongue lapping us up.

*

Kit's driving and I'm dozing with one foot out the window, dreaming about being forced to eat small rocks that are actually gelatin, when I wake up because the car's stopped, engine off.

"Are we outta gas?"

"No, I just…took a detour." Kit grins, looking past me out the window.

The sun's starting to dim and lower. I pull myself up through the sunroof and look around like the turret of a tank. We're on a dirt road flanked by rows of clapboard buildings the same color as the dirt. Their porches sag into the road like wide tongues hanging out of mouths, railings and posts leading up to same-sagging skeletons of awnings and the upper arches of facades reaching high. The buildings all have several boards missing from their sidings, some walls bearing holes, but I can't tell if the holes came from something trying to get into or out of the buildings. There's a breeze and I think I hear creaking. Most of the windows I can see are cracked or missing, and what window panes have stayed are coated in gray dust. Outside the buildings, there's no detritus of human life—no evidence. Our Honda is the newest thing here.

"There was a sign," Kit says. "It's a *ghost town*."

In the fading light, the dirt road leads into hills that darken into each other, into what might be a dead end.

"What kind of sign?" I ask. "Blue or brown?"

"Brown." She raises an eyebrow. Brown means it's a state thing, an officially recognized yet likely not-attended-to joint. "Of course, the sign didn't say 'ghost town' outright," she says, "but, you know, jargon, codes." She starts to get out. "It's a jackpot."

My eyes fix on a building on our left, behind Kit, with triangles of curling ironwork like cobwebs in the corners where posts meet porch roof. The windows and doors are boarded up completely. The letters F E _ D are still nailed to its front, a sun-bleached phantom shape filling in the other E. I slide back down and crouch in the passenger seat. My heel slips into a crack in the vinyl.

"Ethical?" I ask. We haven't done it this way before, going to a grave-yard or someplace haunted. My stomach tumbles, internal turbulence.

Her brow furrows at me.

"I mean it just feels like…hunting at a zoo, or something," I say. "A little too fish-in-a-barrel." My mouth feels grainy, like I ate something too sweet, and I can't pull my eyes off the dark windows of the buildings, some kind of magnetism gripping my eyes, my mouth, my stomach. The road feels narrower.

"You think this is a ghost zoo? No. Whatever's here hasn't been caged, hasn't been hunted down. We don't even deal in *ghosts*, Gloria, you know that. This is just a place of saturation." Her tone is annoyed, but coaxing.

I don't know what to say next but it doesn't really matter because something about the road distorts and the faces of the buildings yawn open like mouths and I have to quick open my door and vomit onto the road. Beany.

"Ah, shit." Kit opens her door and comes around to my side. The keys in the ignition make the open door beep morse code for H, for Honda. I don't like putting the sound into such an empty place, a place I don't think wants us in it. I feel like an interloper.

Kit puts her hand on my forehead and her palm feels warm, the fingers cool. I'm glad she knows how to do mother-gestures sometimes. I heave forward into her hip and burp. Kit catches what breath she can in a jar she snags from the backseat. Later I'll make a label: APPREHEN-SION (ABOUT EXPLOITING A DESERTED DESERT TOWN).

I spit onto the road, catch my breath. The rancid taste brings up a memory.

"Kit, I hadn't thrown up in twelve years," I say. "Remember? It was at your birthday party."

"Well, it was after the party. And we decided to go to a skating rink even though we thought we were getting too old."

"Oh yeah, it was just us and a bunch of little kids we didn't know. And I—"

"You spun too much and puked right on the rink," she laughs, "and some of them skated through it and fell down, right in your puke."

I laugh and lean my cheek against the car door. "We ran out and Bonnie was waiting for us in the station wagon, motor running, like she knew we needed a getaway. And I ate more cake when we got home."

Kit hadn't been mad that I'd puked on her birthday. We're quiet for a moment as the memory settles around us.

"And now we're here and you've ended your streak." She sighs, but I can't tell if it's tired or disappointed. She takes a half step back from me and looks down the road, some plan forming in her brain.

I wait a little while before I say, "Sorry I puked on you, Ghost Town."

Kit paces, one hand rubbing her stomach, considering. The buildings have loosened their grip on my senses, but my feeling of intruding remains.

The sky is bruising and Kit says, "We're gonna sleep indoors tonight."

"Inside the car's indoors," I say.

"Nope. Real doors. Walls. Floorboards. Inside. Don't you miss houses?"

"Do *you?*"

"It's been a while—they're here—we're here—why not? Cheaper and closer than a motel."

"No way. I think we should get back in the car, drive somewhere else. Like into tomorrow."

INVENTORY: Kit's pulling our blankets out of the backseat, the boxy yellow flashlight, peanut butter and Saltines. All these things that feel like part of me. She fills her arms, says, "Grab Bonnie. We'll go to that small one on the end."

I get Bonnie's jar from between the seats and hold it against my chest. Blue shades of night are swallowing up everything around us. "Kit," I call, "I have some serious heebie-jeebies about this."

She keeps walking away, flashlight beam dancing ahead of her, and jingles the keys over her head.

I think about what might be inside, about what the dark might be concealing, about what makes the ghost of the ghost town, about what's worse: outside and alone, or inside and with this sister?

I walk toward her, say, "Will you just tell me what's going on, why you want to do this?"

"Didn't you feel it when you threw up?"

"Yeah, I felt terrible, what does—"

"Wait—I felt it but you didn't?" she says. "Interesting."

"*What?*"

"This vibration! It was like a rubber band had been plucked, stretching between *your* stomach and *that* building." She jabs her thumb over a shoulder. The whites of her eyes glinting.

I hadn't felt it. Maybe too busy feeling sorry and creeped out about barging in here. I hadn't noticed the building Kit's headed toward, like all the other buildings were hiding it.

We walk down the road, Kit has one arm loaded with our stuff and holding the flashlight, the other stretched out to her side, hand in line with my stomach, feeling some current, I guess. I assess my insides: numb and deflated.

The building she leads us to is a narrow A-frame, porchless, worn. Dirt packed between grooves in the wood. The door has four panes of glass neck-high. Kit tries the knob. It rattles, squeals through corrosion, but doesn't open. She tries again, leaning into it with one foot pushing against the door frame; we hear a *schink* and she pushes a little harder. The bolt breaks inside and the door opens.

"Oh look at that," Kit says. "Just had to encourage the disintegration."

We step inside, flashlight on, and my head fills with stale smells and dust. Our circle of light reveals a wooden floor, exposed beams in the slanting ceiling, a long low table on the left side, a tall cabinet against the back wall, and to the right: ghosts. I freeze and Kit lets in a small gasp, but she steadies the light so we can see the rack of draping, long, white garments, swaying in the push of air we brought in. This place is small enough that Kit just reaches her arm out and touches them, rubs the fabric between her fingers. I'm clinging to her back, jars of Bonnie and peanut butter wedged between us by my arm, and I can see little pleats, scalloped edges, no waistlines. Long sleeves.

"Are those…nightgowns?" I ask.

"Hmmmm," says Kit. "What was going on in here?" She closes the door behind us.

A moth flies out from between the folds, draws toward the flashlight. Now that we're inside, I think, I don't feel like I'm going to throw up, I don't feel like I'm being swallowed.

"Do you feel anything?" I ask her.

"A humming, in the air. Do *you* feel anything?"

"Nothing. But, different from what I felt out there."

Kit spreads a blanket on the floor and we settle our bodies down on it, flashlight beaming up between us. We make dry sandwiches with the crackers, eat them slow. I try to keep quiet. I try to ignore the tension in my muscles.

"So we were outside," Kit says, voice low, "and you were sick, stomach emptied, and now we're inside, and you feel okay, and you're filling your stomach." She says this like a kind of math.

I look up, wobble the flashlight around the peak of the ceiling. Thin silver lines looping and crawling, like slug tracks, or some kind of map. Celestial.

"I don't know what to tell you, Kit. I don't know why you felt something connected to me and I didn't. Maybe the scorning feeling I had got puked out and then you could sense it?" I chew. "Tell me about the humming you felt."

"It kind of is like…what you remember feeling right before something important happens. The feeling you have before that you only realize after—the feeling that comes before the car crashes, or before you meet someone you might fall in love with, or before someone else says exactly what you're thinking—a premonitory feeling, but very small, and quiet. That vibration between layers of thought. *That* hum."

I'm surprised she knows it so well. "Did you feel it before Bonnie died?"

Kit puts her hand on the jar of ashes, runs her finger around the gold lid. She looks at me, says, "No." Says, "I think *she'd* been feeling it for years. Maybe even since we were born." Kit lies down, hefts the jar up and holds it over her ribs. "That's what kept her from being afraid of dying, you know? Bonnie isn't in here. I mean, she is, but she isn't. She knows that. We know that. I think it's partly why she wanted us to learn how to feel these things, so we could recognize them without being thrown off by them."

The calf drifts into my mind. I wonder if I'm remembering feeling what Kit's talking about, or if I'm superimposing a memory. The calf makes an ache in my heart and a seizing along my nerves. Am I thrown off by this feeling, this new wanting? I was already thrown off by loss; the possibility of a new *having* is strikingly weighted in the aftermath of that. I look at Bonnie's jar and the diminishing ashes and would like to label it LONGING.

"It's awful being so far away from her," I say.

We are quiet in the awfulness for a while.

"As much as she wanted to be everywhere—" Kit says, "'don't bury me and keep me in one place' and all that—and as much as we wondered what invisible spirit might have rushed out the moment she died, too quick to catch, I do wonder if she's been fully freed."

"Like if she really is all in the jar, in the ashes?"

"Like if it's what she expected it to be, I guess. And if any part of her feels caught. She was devoted to the hidden world—bodiless, intangible, transcended things. Believing she's part of that now, I do reckon there's part of her that's still tied to this world so long as it's within the confines of this jar."

I'm surprised to hear Kit questioning this. Usually her lack of doubt feels powerful enough to capture.

"I wonder what it'll feel like when the jar is empty. To have none of her left."

"Maybe she really will feel everywhere."

We are quiet in the possibility for a while.

"I wonder what this place will look like in the morning," I say.

"All will be revealed," Kit says. She puts the jar on the floor between us. "Isn't that right, Bonnie?"

Curled under blankets, I grab Kit's hand, think about sleeping.

I wake up before her. Gray light's floating in through the window. There's a big black sewing machine in the corner I hadn't noticed last night. I switch off the flashlight. Kit's hair streaks over her face, moves with her breath. I look up and can't see the silver trails on the ceiling anymore. Our feet point toward the cabinet. Wood painted black, still holding patches of lacquer. Two long doors with small tarnished brass knobs, no keyhole. I feel a sudden boldness, being the only non-stilled thing here. Trying to keep quiet, I get up, stand in front of the cabinet. It's taller than I am and legless, its full weight resting on the floor. My hand reaches for a knob, turns it right, and it goes more than I expected. There's a thin sound of the latch drawing back and the doors groan faintly but swing open easy. Kit makes no waking sounds behind me.

INVENTORY OF CABINET: five shelves, lined with jars. My blood zings in my veins. They're uniform in size and shape, neckless, unlabeled. I count six on each shelf, all holding a murky yellow-green liquid and floaty white forms. I lean in closer. Layers of white peeling off a denser mass in one, white and gray spheres at the bottom of another. A pile of white rubbery ribbon. A tangle of pale roots surrounding a bone. One that looks like cloud.

I catch stripes of my reflection on the jars. I close the doors.

*

Outside, I feel jumpy and follow Kit while she tries opening all the doors of the buildings. It feels wrong, like *we could get arrested* wrong, but Kit keeps moving and says we have no intention of stealing or vandalizing and also no one else is here so we don't need to worry. We look through all the windows and all the stuff of the town appears mid-life, like it hasn't been put away or hidden, more like everyone had paused in what-ever they were doing—changing shoes, measuring out tinctures, bagging feed—and whatever made them pause took them away. Short coils of black hair ring around a barber's chair. There are no placards anywhere describing what this place is or what may have happened. Maybe the state doesn't even know. The calf at least had a tiny bit of origin story, but this place is a total mystery as to what caused the mass exodus and how hasty it may have been. I wonder if it had anything to do with the jars in the cabinet, and decide not to tell Kit about them.

We find a water pump and pump it until the brown water turns clear. The fact that we can move it at all means either A: the town is more recently deserted than we thought, or B: the State makes sure some things stay working in case some desert-wandering lunatics stumble into it about to perish. The water tastes like pipe.

We go back to the building we slept in to gather the rest of our stuff, make sure we left no crumbs. Kit rubs a smudge of Bonnie into the threshold. I walk down the road to go wait in the Honda, weaving in and out of the shadows of the buildings. I think about other ghost towns in the state, wonder if they're all the same type of ghosts—people who didn't leave when they should have or could have, buildings and objects impregnated with that knowledge of abandonment or missed opportunity.

A piece of cottonwood fluff skips across the windshield. A figure dressed in flowing white moves down the road in my direction. I start the car and throw it in reverse before realizing I can't abandon Kit, before realizing this person *is* Kit, in one of the long white garments. Goddammit.

I lean out the window. "What the hell are you doing?"

She holds up a jelly jar, facets glinting in the sun.

I feel like there will be a thin layer of something—perhaps ectoplasm—when she takes the dress off. I decide to wait it out. Kit sits in front of what was maybe a post office, white dress tented by her bent legs. She holds the jar in her lap and closes her eyes.

Things stay still. No breeze goes through the ghost town. I suppose time continues to pass; shadows move in the sun's wake. Eventually, Kit slumps forward a bit and carefully screws the lid onto the jar. She gets up and starts peeling off the white dress—no visible residue on her skin or clothes. I start the car again. She lays the dress flat in the middle of the road. We drive in silence.

*

The next rest stop isn't for 15 miles, but we can't wait that long so I pull over. While I pee behind a rock, looking into the horizon, I have a sudden fear that Kit will drive off without me. What does it mean for us to depend on each other? I try to push the thought out of my mind, concentrating on that wavering lead-colored line between the ground and sky and I think *that's where I can exist.*

*

No matter how much you love your Honda, your sister, your landscape, you will eventually feel trapped inside these things, even just for a moment. The past that you have known begs for you to crawl inside it again, to chew on its edges, to melt back into it. Even though it's a disappeared thing, existing only in slight consequence and memory, even though you are sitting still while moving through the atmosphere at 75 mph, racing toward the future where anything's allowed. Proceed with abandon.

*

Tonight we splurge on a motel room. The door is aqua with two locks; the bed is a double and covered with a musty lime-green spread. There's a boxy TV on the dresser and a wall-mounted bottle opener in the bathroom. A landline phone next to a digital alarm clock radio—everyday things everyone can recognize. I turn on the A/C and Kit turns the knobs for the bathtub. Wind and water, harnessed by different tubes and pipes. I kneel in front of the A/C and try to make the machine breeze fill my nose the way the real wind can on certain overpasses spanning rivers, but it's not strong enough.

In the dark, trying to sleep. In close quarters I can smell our bodies. Somehow almost sweet, a curved scent, and something about it would be less repulsive if she wasn't my sister. As if because I love her, I have to love this smell too. As if a secret part of my brain is trying to alert me that I smell the same. Turn off, nose. Close the tap, let me sleep. We aren't even twins, but still—her body so much like mine that I accumulate a feeling of being surrounded by myself too much, confusing the observation with the experience. A tangle of identities. I'm bothered by how alike we are and yet I cannot explain this to her, to discover if she feels the same. Perhaps because I couldn't stand it—to feel the same about this as well.

In the morning I wake up and her limbs are around me. I get out of bed abruptly as I can—I don't care if it wakes her up this time. My chest, having just been restricted by her arms, fills with breaths of disgust. And it's sad, being aware of this happening. This cleaving, or desire for it. I force down some instant coffee (complimentary), go into the bathroom and turn on the shower, but I still feel too close to her, as if she is floating between the molecules filling the windowless bathroom. I feel selfish and tired and the opposite of lonely. An emotional claustrophobia is blooming, taking up space in my chest. I can't look at my face in the mirror, can't bear any resemblances. I hope we see another face today so I can shake this feeling.

*

We're set up on the side of the road, a couple miles away from a gas station, not quite on empty. It could be hours before anyone drives by, but we aren't in any kind of hurry. I'm posted by the open trunk, making sure the sign doesn't blow over and keeping my distance while this morning's trapped feeling dissipates. Kit's wandering around with an open jar, feeling for anything in the air.

I shift my weight from one leg to the other and back and the wind blows my hair over and away from my face. On the other side of the road is a herd of deer, distance making them look about the size of jackrabbits. I study them, checking for deviations like the calf's, but they all look four-legged and single-bodied. Down the road, a car emerges from the heat ripple. Under the speed limit. A black Cadillac with lots of chrome slows even more and stops, on the road, in front of me. The tinted passenger window rolls down, smooth, and the driver's pale, bony hand waves at me. It glows against the black interior, long yellowy nails like claws.

"Halloooo!" she calls.

I bend down and look in. It's just her in there, wearing giant sunglasses so I can only see the lower half of her face, glowing like her hand, with a smile outlined in black lipstick and wrinkles.

"Uh, hello."

"Car problems, sweetie?"

I hold up our sign. "No, just ah, working." I wonder if Kit would call it working?

She reads the sign out loud and slow and her voice is hoarse but velvety, like the dark of the car.

"So what is it—face creams or home-canned vegetables?" she asks.

"Oh, actually, it's invisible things. Can I interest you in a CROW SOUL, or some VOID, some RUMBLE?"

Inside the Cadillac the mouth droops, opens. "You know what, hon? I'm really more looking for something homegrown. But good luck with your little...business." The hand flaps its claws at me and the window rolls up. The Cadillac creeps off.

Kit comes walking back, jar still open. "I don't think this is a very good spot," she says.

*

We see a sign for The Supple Lizard Nude Ranch, the tails of each *p* crossed to imply the ♀, arms outstretched, and we decide to turn left in the next 25 miles because we, too, want to warm our blood in the sun.

"*Supple* makes it sound like a lizard with breasts, though," Kit says, and we wonder if such a creature would have two or six or twenty. I say, "I guess it depends on how many young are in a brood," and then we wonder about that particular aspect of evolution until we make the left turn. The driveway's a couple miles in and leads to a ring of adobe buildings, like a fort.

The girl at the entrance building—nude except for freckles and a sun hat that says LIZARD on a band around the crown—tells us admission to the ranch is an item of knit clothing.

"It gets unraveled and wound into this giant ball behind the complex," she says. "Years and years of shed skins, you know? You can go see it if you want to."

I turn in a pair of wool socks (clean but pilling) and Kit gives up a cardigan with big holes under each armpit, long ago handed down from Bonnie. Right now we're just eager to sprawl out in the sun. We put our other things in an orange locker and walk out, slightly shivery and slow, to a broad slab of red rock.

Off a ways in the distance, past fleshy blobs of other sunbathers, I can see where the clothes go: tucked inside a primitive shack with three walls and a roof is a massive ball of wound threads. The threads are laid on the ball so intricately, an array of colors and weights. In the sunlight it looks like the whole spectrum of color. Someone steps out from behind it—a spry-looking nude woman, gray hair in a topknot, winding a line of yarn from a yellow sweater unraveling in her hands. The ball is nearly twice as tall as she is. All that shed clothing, all that freed skin.

"Super supple," Kit grunts, climbing on the rock.

"I'd suggest we start driving around naked, but—vinyl seats," I say. Rusty dust coats our bodies in the places that press against the rock. We stretch out like cats. Lizard cats. I close my eyes against the sun and the calf's glassy eyes flash in my mind, bright inside like fiery opals. I wonder if this is hypnosis. I wonder what the calf is doing right now, if anyone else is ogling her with their unworthy and unappreciative eyes.

*

In praise of being nude: when your laundry isn't hanging off your body like so much loose skin; when the movement of your legs isn't restricted by the four-way seam between them or by the cut of your skirt; when your armpits only rub against themselves; when a drip of sweat rolls freely, sweetly, from the nape of your neck to the top of your ass; when your birthday suit feels as good as your best birthday and it unfolds itself in offering to the sun—that free feeling, that pre-fruit of knowledge feeling, that brain disconnected but really just unburdened, unencumbered, un-self-conscious feeling, realizing that naked is the best outfit and no wonder animals tend to look so comfortable. No one worries about underwear lines when there are no lines except for where your muscles and joints and fat parts and sagging places press into each other. There are no concave lines on the body—everyone is pushing out, out, out, all over, and the nude body remembers to take up as much space as it pleases. It pleases.

*

Like a herd of mustangs in the distance, four motorcyclists thunder up the Supple Lizard's driveway, dismount and de-helmet, turn in their t-shirts and ramble over with just their leather jackets draped across their shoulders, like capes. As they come closer to us, turning toward each other to talk while they walk, I see the back of one jacket painted with a ropy script: *The Calamity Janes*. They're all at least six feet tall but each with a different proportion of leg to torso, hips to shoulders, muscle to fat. They arrange themselves on the boulder next to us and we all say "Hey." Enough distance to stay strangers or start conversation. They each fold up their jacket and put it under their butt or their head. Smart.

"Gosh, my ass sure is tired," says the one with a scraggly brown braid.

"Where'd you all come in from?" Kit asks.

"California," says the blonde one, "near Death Valley."

34

"And we're goin' all the way to Annie Oakley!" says the one with a gold hoop between her nostrils.

"*Our old gal in the ground!*" they cheer and let out some whoops. They all laugh, and I can't not laugh with them. The tallest one, lying behind Braid, nudges her foot onto Braid's shoulder. Her toenails are red and Braid scratches her instep for her. I think this must have to do with the communication you have to learn when you're vulnerable on the road—balancing on a bike, inside a helmet. I wonder if Kit and I could hack it.

Watching them is like looking through a window at a family, at a pack of animals in their natural habitat. The way they adjust their bodies on the rocks or touch each other when speaking—those gestures of intimacy only noticed by an outsider. Their comfort in territory.

Kit and I introduce ourselves. The one with red toenails says her name is Jo, points to each of the others: Braid is Enza, the blonde is LA, and the one with the nose ring is Terra. This roll-call seems like something they do somewhat regularly.

I ask if one of them is related to Annie Oakley or what the draw is. LA hoots and says, "Nah, we're just disciples of a sort, fashioning lives wherein we get to do what we want, et cetera."

"I think Annie was the end of her family line, anyway?" Jo says.

"Ain't that just the way," Enza laughs.

"We named ourselves after Calamity Jane but we look up to Annie just as much, even if she was a little more… polished," Jo says.

"You think she was polished?" asks Terra.

"Polished enough to have a musical written about her, at least," says Jo.

"Probably a little more respected by certain men," Terra clarifies.

"Which I maintain neither Annie nor Jane cared about," Enza says. "If you know what I mean."

"Certainly do," Jo says. She points her thumb back at Enza and looks at us, says, "They've always had a strong hunch about what lesbian lives may have been lost to history."

Enza rolls onto their stomach, feet kicking up behind, "I just think they would've made a real sweet couple, even if it was an on-and-off thing."

The rest of the group agrees.

"It's a long haul to Ohio," LA says, "but Annie did a lot of touring, too—she and Jane both did—shooting their names all over the map. They would've had motorcycles, too, if they could. Shoot."

"Yeah, something light and snappy for Annie," Jo says.

"Anything for a quicker getaway, huh?" LA rolls her eyes. "She didn't need that, though."

"As far as we *know*," Terra says.

LA looks at us. "These two have this theory that Annie was something of a criminal in her 'spare time,' I guess—"

"Actually," Terra says, "I've changed my theory. I now think she was skilled enough to pull off what you might call 'sleight of gun,' wherein she figured out how to use her tricks for pickpocketing." Terra turns her smug face toward the sun.

Jo says, "I'm sticking with my 'heavily disguised bank robber' theory—she had the gun confidence to pull that off in spades."

"I thought her suit was hearts," Kit pipes in, clever, remembering for me Annie's trick of shooting the card right in the heart from an impressive number of paces.

Jo enjoys this, her eyes leveling up the two of us. "Where are you two staying tonight?" Jo asks. "Seemed like there was only one motel around these parts."

Kit and I look at each other, she opens her mouth so her bottom teeth show. "In our car, somewhere," she says.

Jo and the others take turns locking eyes with each other, then Jo says, "Why don't you stay with us tonight? We'll have plenty of room—ended up getting the biggest beds available."

This is so appealing I say "Yes" without even looking at Kit, but by the time I say the *s* I hear her saying it, too.

"Great," LA says, smiling.

We talk more about roadkill, old billboards, how they navigate the road as a group and their route to Ohio. Then we all just kind of shut up and get to lazing. In such close proximity to bodies neither mine nor Kit's, I can't help but stare at them. They look like poems, the way LA's tendons show just behind her knees and wrists, the way Terra's tawny shoulders fade down into pale breasts and paler ribs, the way their bodies are so relaxed they might be melted, bending to the will of the sun. All this makes me realize how tense I feel in my own body, the clench of watching, and I concentrate on relaxing my muscles from the feet up, feeling my flesh ease itself onto the rock even more, ease itself into the presence of these other bodies, into the presence of itself.

I think of how a body is an abstract container. For organs, for thoughts. So often covered up and therefore a mystery, everyone's obviously-concealed secret walking itself around all day. Each one is different but more or less in the same way. Flesh folds the same, hairs crosshatch predictably. The mystery comes from how it belongs to someone.

The veins on the tops of my feet and hands plump in the sun as they warm; fields of goosebumps crop up on my thighs and belly as the breeze passes through. We're an array of rolls of fat, planes of muscle coming together in a body cartography, colored by sunburn and levels of melanin, each with our unique constellations of moles and spots, each marked with scars tiny and large. One on my hip like a crescent moon, from gashing myself on a rock in the river. The place where Kit had to have stitches on her elbow after using it to break into the house after locking herself out. Scars with ink in them: a cobra with a fat rose for a hood on Terra's back. Horseshoes on the bottoms of Jo's feet. Flowers blooming out of LA's shoulders, bluebirds swooping between her shoulder blades. Enza's skin scattered with symbols and pictograms made of thin black lines. A small, simple open eye Kit poked over her breastbone one night a few years ago. Bodies with pictures.

I'm watching the breeze moving the spindly branches of the tree behind our rock, directing them in no real pattern. The most delicate chaos. Then I notice a line of blood running down the red rock from between Terra's bent legs, bringing a truer red to the land's red—both iron, and the rock admits it is only a kind of orange. She reaches to her butt—brushing it like maybe a bug's on her, I suppose—then holds her fingers up so she can see. "Dang," she says. "The old curse."

I remember Bonnie saying: "Like a goddamn self-cleaning oven."

*

We're clothed and getting ready to drive to the motel and I know if I don't ask now I may never get the chance and have the nerve at the same time again:

"Can I ride on the back of someone's bike?"

LA hands me her helmet. It's heavier than I expected and makes me feel disproportioned but safe as we both straddle her old gray BMW. She clamps my arms around her ribs and then we're going down the road, I'm part of this pack, I've never felt this kind of free and I think it must be close to flying. Strands of her hair whip against my face, I'm shot through with wind, the air fills my nose on its own, and the colors of the landscape run together more than they do through the windshield. I shout my amazed thanks into LA's ear and feel her ribs bounce like she must be laughing. We lean together through the wide curves. She's so sure of her moves, her muscles controlling the machine. I wish I could put this in a jar.

*

I feel like it's the first time I've been properly inside for weeks, in this room: turquoise and olive diamond-patterned wallpaper, matching bed-spreads on two queens, brass and Lucite fixtures, two chairs covered in dark orange velour. A picture above the bed shows a pack of wolves in a field, jaws agape and pointing moonward. We're all sitting around in towels, clean and damp, and I'm imagining us from up above: wrinkly dollops of pastel colors, arms reaching like ferns unfurling for the bounty of food (tacos, churros, oranges, rellenos) in the middle of one of the beds. Something like synchronized swimming in our movements.

I'm warm and clean and my insides are glowing like a lantern. When we all pulled up to the motel, Kit paused at the trunk of the Honda, put a hand on the closed lid, and put her arm around me while we walked inside. Now she has a taco in each hand, laughing with a full mouth, and for now neither of us need to be anxious about what will happen next. A safety in numbers type thing.

Terra and Jo are trying to tell a story about being run out of a tiny town last year in Arizona, locals who didn't take kindly to their bikes or their brazenness; they're laughing over each other's impersonations of the outraged barkeep. LA seems to be dozing off except she takes a sip of her beer every now and then. I almost let myself start wondering what they'd be capable of—if they'd rob a bank, make a living pickpocketing, if Annie Oakley's grave isn't their only reason for continuous movement. But the indulgence of enjoying this day, this night, their wealth of ca-maraderie is stronger than my impulse to worry. Enza gets up and paws through their bags, pulls out a camera. Taps my shoulder and says, "Let me take your picture."

Enza's fingers are curled around the body of the camera, an old Olympus. The fingernails are chewed down, a few knuckles laced with thin red cuts like they'd been rooting around in brambles. Right thumb winds the film to the next frame.

"What do you want me to do?"

"Pose for your mugshot." They smile and one eye squints closed.

Half a nervous laugh. "What are the charges?"

"Oh, *you know*," they say, lifting the camera in front of their face, adjusting the lens.

38

I settle my back against the wall, think of what I'd be taken in for, think of a heroic deed that would merit arrest, think of the calf trapped behind glass. The camera clicks, cranks to a new frame. I lift my chin and look into the lens. Click.

"Perfection," Enza says. "I like to do this with a lot of the people we connect with. Says a lot about a person. Kit, you're up."

Kit rolls off the bed and I sit down to watch her, half listening to Jo and Terra. Kit brushes her hair back, relaxes her face into a slight frown, and I have no idea what she's picturing as the shutter clicks. I think of my face wound up in the company of others I'll never see, my face looking like I don't know what exactly, safely rolled away and undeveloped in Enza's camera for who knows how long, how far.

In the morning, we part ways in the parking lot, gulping down cruddy lobby coffee from paper cups; Kit and I say thanks for sharing their room. We all shake hands and then they get on their bikes and they roar off, Jo leading, Enza last, reaching up to wave at us. Kit and I get in the Honda, which now feels cushy and quiet, and we turn out of the parking lot in the opposite direction.

*

I drive steady for a long time and then I'm back in the saddle of claustrophobia, the trapped-in feeling. I give into it, accelerate and feel the steady shake of our mechanics. I'm Bullitt, I'm Kowalski, Captain America, I'm every horse in the race trying to get out from under the jockey, fire blasting from my lungs, only concerned with speed as a means of breaking free and I become a whole herd of horses, unbridled, unshod, only the body that knows how to run run run up up up up up—if only I could run and drive at the same time, if only my body could produce the same power and push on its own so maybe I would stop feeling like my muscles were going to wrench themselves away from the joint and writhe out of my skin, the meat of me tearing itself free. Restlessness makes me animal.

I think of how the calf is fixed, static. A stillness. A demand to stop, to stay. Frozen in brazen animal glory, needing nothing.

*

"Kit," I say. Another night in the Honda, silver starlight pouring through the sunroof. I've got the driver's seat reclined and she's stretched out as much as possible in the back seat.

"Mm."

"Kit, I need something. We need to go back for something."

"Did you leave your wallet at the last truck stop or what."

"No, I mean, we need to go further back. Kit, I'm in love and I need to collect what I am in love with."

"Where are we, anyway?" She yawns. "Everything looks so different at night."

"We're a couple hundred miles from where I want to be."

"I keep waking up every morning thinking I've been transported in my sleep," she says. "Where do we want to be?"

I count our cash, pull my seat up, put my shoes on, start the car and get us moving. Kit mumbles about the dashboard lights reflecting on the windows like a space ship. Soon the sun starts creeping up and Kit, fully awake, climbs in the front passenger seat. I explain while keeping my eyes on the road: I'm possibly seeking the opposite of an invisible in a jar; I am identifying with an oddity, wanting a strange creature, singular yet split, as a rule of life, whatever that may mean; I have a great compassion and curiosity to find out if love can resurrect anything left in this creature (I imagine a slick mass wobbling toward me on two four six eight legs—my darling!); I have a very strong magnetic attraction which will possess my body and cause me to drive back; you can't rationally explain love.

"Hold up, sister," she says. "You want to do this in the daytime? What's even the point if you're just gonna get caught?"

I lift my foot off the gas. I realize I haven't thought it through yet.

PART II

When we—I grind my feet into the dirt—*last left*—push my right fist, thumb extended, toward the road—*our hero...*

No cars, no cars, no cars.

*

My brain (my heart) is a spool that has let out a slack-line along the road since becoming attached to the calf.

My other half? Half-calf. Decaf. Halved, calved. A calf-eteria (an old punchline). Have calf, will travel.

A spool of umbilical cord, maybe. Not sure which one of us has the womb-end.

*

Do you have a plan? Kit had asked.

Searching with my eyes closed and arms out again.

No cars, no cars, a semi passes, no cars.

The afternoon air is warm warmer warmest all around me with breezes cutting through like wonderful knife blades.

Does it help to take steps backwards? Isn't that what they do in movies? While wearing sunglasses and cut-off shorts? When's the last time I watched a movie?

When Kit drove away, there was an audible ripping noise, like bed sheets. That's another movie thing—bed sheets for escape.

*

What is the point of having a plan? I touch my pocket to make sure my thin bundle of ones and fives is still safe, as if it would've blown away somehow. Plans hardly ever work anyway. Here's a plan, Kit: hurry up. Meet me with a melted milkshake. Greet my calf with some genuine mirth. Try to see her as I do. See her as I see me.

I wonder where Kit is. I try not to wonder where I am. I am on a line surrounded by landscape; sometimes there are signs, I know there will be a car, and this is placement enough.

Three cars pass, going the other direction. If I crossed and stood on the other side of the road, would I realize it? What is this a sign of?

*

45

I think about riding with LA however many days before, how covering distance like that felt so different from riding in a car. Like I could see myself as a moving black dot on a map, route dictated by terrain rather than highway. And the loudness was terrifying at first, then immersive.

*

The calf, the calf, my calf. My heart throbs, I can feel my pulse in my fist. I think of my love as some kind of holy grail, sacred, but not untouchable. Do objects long for us when we aren't there? (Does the Honda miss me, maybe?) If it was once alive—or parts of it were—is it really an object? When is that transference?

A wind, a wind, a beautiful green Buick Skylark pulls over, I remember where I'm trying to be going.

*

I shut the door and—

"I'm Betty," says the driver, a woman with a high tight gray perm, maybe early fifties.

"I'm Gloria." My mouth is dry.

She jabs her thumb toward the backseat, "That's Mom," she says.

Mom is a piebald Great Dane, white and rust like a cow, sleeping all over the back seat, with her pink belly looking at me.

"Mo—"

"Where you headed?" Betty asks.

"Northeast, I guess, toward Fort Sumner. How about you?"

"We're goin' north, too—but west. That place with all the satellites? Very Large Array? That's where Mom and I like to go camping. Inn't that right, Mom?"

Mom yawns and licks her muzzle, rolls over.

I think about what Kit would think of that place, about what could be reached, what would want to be reached, if it's like any of the non-living entities we seek or if they would be seeking us, looking to contain us. And then—

INVENTORY: no jars, that's for damn sure. No Bonnie, either.

"So, what're you doin' out here on your own?"

I think, *Where do I begin?* I realize I haven't been in a car without Kit for a long, long time. I take in the faded brown vinyl of the dashboard, the gearshift knob worn from years of palming, the sun-bleached alien figurine bobbing from the rearview with a disproportionately large head, shiny black eyes, and string-bean fingers offering a peace sign.

"Trying to rendezvous with my sister," I say, "after I pick something up in Fort Sumner. You get this in Roswell?" I tap the alien's foot.

"Yep—lived there about nine years now, haven't seen anything like *that* yet. Some other things, though. UFOs, space specters, that sort of thing, but no hard alien evidence yet." She thumps her fist on the steering wheel.

Kit and I went to Roswell once, as adults—we'd been taken there as kids on the few milestone journeys to Carlsbad Caverns. All the once-bright green aliens in shop windows at kid-height were faded and dusty, and the dioramas in the UFO museum were garish and cobbled together. Mannequins dressed as doctors and FBI agents gathered around a make-shift alien on a gurney, all magic and tension stripped from a moment of high speculation and wonder. I think it must have struck us differently than other visitors who were sci-fi fans or believers, disappointed in the lack of pizzazz and proof. For us, it was a frozen moment of discovery and exploration, coming face to face with something that had only been supposed—never proven—and the tension of that moment, the energy that would allow the future to go one way or the other, was sucked out by static figures and fluorescent lights.

Perhaps this was expecting too much from a small-town tourist at-traction.

"…of course, their radar picked it up on July fourth, so we can't put too many eggs in that basket. But I think all those satellites are pickin' up on things and not even telling the computers, or operators—the satellites are keeping secrets."

I catch up. "What, like an artificial intelligence conspiracy?"

"Sure, or, they're being manipulated by whoever it is they're inter-cepting. They're just big eavesdroppers, y'know. Just big ears. So Mom and I go out a few times a year to see if we can pick up on anything, too."

"Have you heard anything yet?"

"Heck, you think even a dog's ear would be able to reach way way *way* up into space and catch those waves?"

"Well, I—"

"I'm sorry, sweetie, I meant eavesdrop and ears like *sense*, for us." She pauses, drums her thumbs on the steering wheel, swerves around the bloating body of an unidentified furry thing. "You know how sunflowers, let's say, follow the sun with their faces all day?" She steers with her knees a beat so she can frame her face with her hands and move it left and right.

"I think it's like that. The satellites move based on the force of something else—literally a higher power, but without all the theology, let's say."

"I thought they moved based on a computer program, controlled by humans."

"What do you think tells the humans what to do?" She clicks her tongue and points a finger gun at me. The gesture of a cracked code. I'm not too sure what she's talking about or if I'm asking the right questions, but I don't mind being on this side of the conversation with someone who believes in something like this—space-based and invisible in its own way. Mom shifts herself onto her belly and settles her head on the armrest between Betty and me. Her eyes beg and she ekes out a whine so thin I'm surprised Betty hears it. "Time to pull over," she says, and the Skylark crunches over the shoulder.

We stretch our legs while Mom ambles around looking for the right patch of pale grass to pee on. I close my eyes and let the sun come through, fleshy red like cherry pulp, flashing lighter and darker as my eyeballs twitch back and forth. It feels safe inside like this, and I start feeling uneasy about what might happen when I open my eyes again.

I start to worry she's going to ask me questions I'm not up to answering, or that her enthusiasm for life in outer space will turn into some sort of proselytizing. I don't want to talk about beliefs. The soul is fine but I don't want so much for man-made words like *good* and *evil* to get involved. It's a worry like I'm harboring a secret. Some folks thought Bonnie was a witch. But that's also a man-made thing, isn't it? What about a feeling, or a memory? Things that happen, that exist but you can't touch them or see them. Not in front of your eyes, anyway. We were concerned with the invisible things, not formed by hands. Things tucked in small vials Bonnie kept in the pocket of her apron along with the pink packets of false sugar.

I open my eyes to see Mom, bounding in near slow motion to Betty's open arms. I feel a pang of longing, look down the highway wide and empty clear to the horizon, feel the choice between two unknowns and decide to get back in Betty's car.

*

"Y'know, I used to hitch rides, back when I lived over in west Texas. It was slow going, given the population and how much space people like to keep between themselves."

"Where were you trying to go?"

48

"Oh, anywhere. This was when I was about twelve, thirteen, just wanted to get out. Never got very far when I did get a ride at all. Once or twice they didn't ask where I was headed and just took me back home. Someone took me to the drive-in one time—I asked if we could go, just to see what would happen—and we drove eight hours, straight across to Beeville. I woke up at The Bronco, I remember it was called—*Vanishing Point*—that car ripping around on this huge screen and the sound of it smashing at the end coming through these crummy little speakers right into the windows. Took me a second to realize it was a movie, that we weren't about to be in a terrible crash. Paralyzed me, y'know? Put me off riding in cars for a bit." A big hero, a big screen, but a bummer of an ending.

"But how'd you get home, then?"

"Well, I stayed awhile. Called my folks, told them I'd found a job which wasn't a lie for too long, then I purloined one of these babies—" she patted the dashboard "—and I had a place to sleep. Waited tables savin' up gas money and made it back to Alpine for my fourteenth birthday. Anyway, how long you been hitchin', Gloria?"

"Gosh, just here and there, when I need a ride and Kit's got the car. Nothing so extreme, really."

"And Kit has the car now, huh?"

"Yeah, but it's just temporary. We never split up for long."

"I see. Y'all trying to get some place by sometime?"

How much rope to let slack? I don't want to come across so rudderless or drifty as the truth might seem. That we go where and when we please; we stay as long as we want or can. That we've been doing this one way or another for longer than we can remember, starting as little kids in the backseat with a box of jars between us for long stretches of blurry road. So I say, "Well, we haven't decided yet. Got a few places in mind we might head to, probably end up gorging ourselves to death in Pie Town and that'll be the end of it." I try to laugh.

Betty leans into the steering wheel and peers into the horizon. "Getting dark ahead," she says. "See 'em? Storm clouds'll be blowin' east, though, lucky for us. Looks like hail."

"How can you tell?" I can hardly see the dark spots in the clouds.

"I can sense it. I've learned." She sits up straight and serious. "Good thing I picked you up. The sky coulda fallen on you."

*

We get caught up behind an ambulance, no sirens on, no flashing lights. I wonder what's happened inside it, especially in this part of the state where the standard for isolation is different. Who's been born in this ambulance? Who's died? Who has *undied*—come back from glimpsing death and what did they think after?

"You give much thought to what'll come after?"

"After."

"Yeah, you know, after you and your sister are done with this—unless, this is it for you, like, this is the rest of your life."

How I want to tuck and roll out the door like a tumbleweed. I say, "We haven't really talked about it yet, I mean, we're still deciding. Don't like to worry too much about the future."

"I didn't say you needed to *worry*, per se." She pauses. "Just wondering how far down the road you wanted to go."

I remember the first time I got lost coming home after a day of driving without any purpose except to get away for a spell, disoriented and hypnotized by sun and asphalt, feeling like all roads looked the same. It was dusk and the sky and the hills and the road were gray and violet; it was too dark to read the non-reflective road signs, no landmarks found or remembered. Frustrated and too thirsty to cry, a quarter-full gas tank, I decided any road would do—any road would eventually lead someplace that either would be fine to park for the night or would have some sort of map or person who knew their directions. So I took a left and drove into darkness for twenty miles, headlights illuminating no human evidence except the road, until they blinked at me in the distance: the unmistakable taillights of a Volvo station wagon. Bonnie's car, headed home from work. The taillights grew brighter as I got closer, her turn signal reminding me where to turn in, and I carefully tailgated my mother down the half-mile driveway. When we both got out of the cars, she said, "'Bout time you remembered where you're from."

I wonder if any road I'd turned onto would've led to the same place.

"I said how far down the road you need me to take you? Gloria?"

I swallow and say, "Can I camp with you and Mom tonight? Please?" I look at her profile and notice the briefest twinge above her eyebrows. A recognition.

And she says, "Of course you can, sweetie. Of course you can."

We drive a while longer until the gold fades from the daylight and Betty tells me to look out for an open flat spot. Soon enough I see a space a ways off the road by a boulder uncrowded by scrubby bushes, and the sparse vegetation is low enough to drive over. The Skylark eases over the shoulder, crawls several yards, and Betty manages a U-turn so the headlights face the highway.

"I only have one tent, but plenty of bedding and it's not too cold tonight. I'd rather you not sleep in the car."

"That's fine—it's been too long since I've spent a night roofless—it'll feel good."

Betty stakes her tent using the Skylark as a windbreak and I kick rocks aside, make a sandwich of blankets. I sit and lay out the inventory of everything I have with me:

One pair each of socks, underwear, shorts, jeans. Thin bundle of cash. The sewing kit. One bar of white soap wrapped in an old gray washcloth. Half-liter water bottle, half-full. A two-blade pocket knife with can opener and corkscrew. The body is dark green engraved with G.O. at one end, but I don't know whose initials those are. And, a sandwich. Kit made me a sandwich, bread and peanut butter, folded an envelope of wax paper around it, tucked it in my pack without telling me.

All these things practically glow with a new quality of both familiarity and foreignness. The objects know they have to step into Kit's role for the moment, and we all know they don't fill it out.

Mom settles down, mostly curled inside the tent. Her hind feet stick out and kick up dust when she scratches an itch. Betty pats the dog's haunch and murmurs something about how she'll keep watch the first shift, like some half-joking deal they have worked out. She sits with a large lantern in front of her, points far east where the sky's faded to glooming blues. "See that little vertical break, way off?"

I squint. I can just make out something like a patch of darker static in the horizon.

"That's the storm," she says.

We watch it move along inch by inch, the clouds passing and depleting themselves over some faraway town or highway or untrod patch of wilderness. I wonder if there's thunder happening way out there. The storm gets smaller and smaller and then is indistinguishable from the rest of the clouds in the distance.

"It's a transmittance from the up to the down," she says. She puts her sunglasses back on and I can't tell where her eyes are looking. "Invisible currents dripping down, if only we're awake and waiting to catch them."

I give in, slightly. Softly, "I know about some invisible things."

"I knew you would. I could tell you knew how to listen when I first saw you off in the distance. Thumb out like an antenna."

The sun's sunk fast and I wrap myself, not unlike a burrito, in the blankets she's lent me. They smell warm like dog paws. "Thank you for the ride, Betty. And thanks to Mom, too."

"You're welcome, sweetie," she says, and slowly dims her lantern.

*

I have a dream of our eternity: mixing handfuls of Bonnie ashes with pump water and eating the paste, glutting ourselves on an ever-replenishing bitter clay of her. I dream this, feeling that wet sand in the mouth, until I throw up in the dream and I wake up sweating. I think I feel my nose bleeding but it's just snot. Something startling about waking up like this makes me feel like crying anyway. A feeling like my body coming unhemmed.

Mom pads over, licks the tears and sweat off my face. I roll over on my back and she circles around me, stepping over my legs and around my head before she settles down and drapes herself across my stomach so our bodies form an X. Her bony ribcage pinches into the softer expanse of me, like she's keeping me from blowing away. Should I stay or should I go? Betty's sunglasses gleam in the moonlight and she's snoring faintly. If I leave them I will be alone again, likely for longer. If I stay I'll be feasting on company and distraction from myself and the scrap of plan I have.

And Kit might miss me when she comes.

There's no exact time or place; I'm just on my own to get my calf and she's just supposed to know when to meet us, being better at keeping track of time. While I search, she sells jars. This is how we multitask. Divide and conquer.

INVENTORY OF A DISCUSSION: Kit, the practical, bases-covered thinker, put her palms on the table. Her nails short-trimmed without much dirt troubling them. My nails chawed and torn at—an expression, a gesture of a mind with no room to pace.

We shared a can of tin-tinged lemonade from the rest stop vending machine. Tiny moths frantically threw themselves at the yellow lights.

"There's that famous church," she said, "up north. The one with the hole."

Bonnie had told us about people stopping at the diner on their way, on their pilgrimage. People with wheelchairs, crutches, walkers, leg braces made of scrap materials. People with eyes that wouldn't open, eyes with reds instead of whites, eyes that flinched in pain when their inner ear heard a devil. People with bodies that refused to heal. The hole was dug into daily for the hurting people—they could wait in line for hours to get a scoop of dirt from a small shovel, or they could buy a baggie of the dirt in the gift shop (it was unclear if one method was more blessed than the other). Nightly, the hole performed the miracle of filling back up—that is, the earth was said to do this, or god via the earth—to replenish what had been given during the day. The church claimed no human involvement.

"Two objectives," she continued. "One: to offer these people an alternative or supplemental aid. I know, we don't capture these invisibles with the idea that they heal or are medicinal, *I know*, but they can still help, potentially, like a prayer or a candle or an affirmation. Salve rather than salvation. I'll set up near the exit—where the people coming out may be disappointed by what the hole doesn't offer or just optimistic and willing to pile on the good luck. Either way, desperate and open to the idea of buying a jar out of a trunk."

"You sound like a swindler," I said in a small voice.

"Then listen: the second objective is to visit this hole myself."

Ever since she'd learned about the hole, she'd been suspicious. Something about the claims set her on edge, but I'm not sure why—Bonnie didn't take issue with it, but she didn't buy it either. To me, the hole of dirt seemed just as plausible as what we were doing, and whether or not you believed didn't stop our jars from having an effect on someone else. I figured the same for the hole. But Kit had some sort of bone to pick. While gathering the soul of a jackrabbit or the sensation of saguaro growth into an olive jar was magical and sometimes unbelievable to many, I wasn't sure what we did could be called a miracle. And unlike the church with the hole, we never claimed it was.

"So while you're chasing after love and reuniting with that calf, I'll be giving that a go, seeing what it does to people, seeing if the hole or its dirt is giving anything off. Or maybe it'll resist being jarred altogether. Or maybe it's just plain dirt. Anyway, I want to keep moving and with the amount of time it should take for both of us to do these things, plus the traveling, I figure I'll be able to meet you."

We planned to split somewhere on 380, a reasonable distance for me to cover walking or hitching while she drove. It made sense for her to take the Honda since she was bringing the stock and supplies with her. It had been a long while since we'd spent so much time apart; deep in the pit of my stomach I was both eager and dreading it. I focused on the eagerness.

*

I wonder what would be in a jar Kit might prescribe to me now. Maybe RATTLESNAKE AIM or PLUMB LINE GRAVITY, something sure of itself. Mom, breathing deeply, draped like an arched bridge over me. I picture a flea on the tip of her snout and another somewhere on her skinny tail, fleas trying to find each other—but do they even know how large this dog is, or what parts of the dog they're on, that they're even on a dog at all? This dog could just stand up and shake them off and walk somewhere else whenever she pleased, for all the fleas knew. Did I get Kit and myself shaken off the dog's back?

No, it seems we are still firmly on the dog.

"All right, Sister Flea," I say to the stars. "May as well suck the blood out of this thing while we can."

I don't think my leaving wakes Betty. Mom circles into the warmth of my blankets on the ground. A wave of cloud moves in front of the moon as soon as I start walking away from the campsite. What leaps to mind in the opaque black is not panic or stumbling (for I step slowly and follow the pull of an inner compass) but rather what I'd seen on the ceiling of that A-frame house in the ghost town. Celestial slug trails like a map, shimmering in the flashlight beam and vanished by morning.

Of course, when we split, one thing we overlooked was who should have the flashlight. And so I am out in the dark, consoling myself that the batteries were faulty anyway.

*

Usually a sister is someone you don't remember meeting. No *A this is B, B this is A* introduction. Just immediate presence and proximity from the Time Before Memory. There-ness. An actual ingredient of your reality. Good luck knowing the world without them.

*

Walking on the rocky ground makes clear the thinness of the soles of my shoes. I feel all the lumps of the earth, practically grip them with my toes. It feels right to walk along the side of the road rather than on it. Keeping some mystery and chance in the steps, a little more natural than what is flattened by paving. A little stumbly but still feeling the compass pull. I can't quite see the rocks and stunted plants in my path but I can hear each step I take, the hushed crunch. The only sound besides my breathing and the microsounds of small night creatures who do their living in the dark, invisible by instinct. Footsteps being sound and feeling connecting into a knowledge, a recognition that each one takes me further forward. My bounty of steps, sum of their parts yet to be seen.

*

Something about walking in the stillness of night makes me feel my blood differently, as if it's flooding my joints and pulling muscles, my body calling itself awake and more than usual. In case. Because, you never know. What lurks in a dark desert. And then my breath chases my blood, quickening and filling, getting ready to spring in whatever darkened direction feels like safety.

The highway stripes are flat little ghosts in the night and I follow alongside them. Like the slug trails, but man-made. I think I am going in the right direction. I walk east toward what looks like the beginning of the sunrise—the sun is my plan, for now. A foothold for the brain.

What is the threat in being alone at night? Or, if this is not still night, before dawn?

All the wild animals, either with paws or in cars, craving the flesh around my bones, reasons for my body to be more afraid than my mind. Walking into hidden places the mind doesn't want to go, led by isolation disguised as boldness. A sudden dark pocket, an emotional tiger trap. Just walk around it, then—but how can you walk around something you can't see the edge of?

And that is how I walk right into it: thoughts of Kit with a broken neck, buckled in the upside-down Honda in a ditch, alone, hungry animals sniffing. Kit with her hands tied out of reach, locked in some maniac's trunk. Kit ignoring the signs and picking up a murderous hitchhiker who has just escaped prison. Kit's body becoming just a body. Kit slipping on the slick floor of a taco joint and cracking her skull open like Bonnie. Kit being arrested for being a public nuisance at the church. Kit joining the church and being indoctrinated by hole-worshippers and not coming back. Kit realizing she's better off without me. Kit not coming back. Me being abandoned in this state that is so much bigger than I am. Bonnie's ashes forgotten somewhere, a strange time capsule.

I keep taking steps while forming this morbid list, steps like the heavy trod of a creature that only arises at night, when fear burns brighter.

Is this what it's like to be invisible? Nobody knows where I am right now or quite where I came from or where I'm going. In this moment I'm just a shadow, walking, seen only by the animals whose eyes see everything with and without daylight. I wonder why Bonnie never compared us to these creatures when trying to explain our similar sense for the unseen—that she didn't describe it as us having such eyes on the inside, capable of blinking onto whatever stirs the ether. The way the eyes of an animal move, darting so confidently, the biological form of the satellites Betty and Mom will greet soon. Seekers seeking seekers, and it takes one to know one.

I made a mistake before Betty went to sleep—didn't ask her where we were, how close we might be to either of our destinations.

As far as I know, none of the terrible fates on my morbid list are happening and my mind clings to this ignorance with a white-knuckled grip and I keep stepping forward, leaving traces of such invisible things behind me like shed skins: doubts of blood, doubts of abandonment, worry of ashes, the tremble in the darkness.

The slowness of going by foot allows time to notice the darkness recede into light in a way my mind mistakes for *suddenly*, after countless steps, though the sun has been rising the whole time and I am indeed walking toward it. Each grain of sand that sits on top of the earth has a shadow growing behind it. I cannot move as quickly as some lizards that skitter at my feet (more heard than seen). Through the twilight of the morning, as the moon sets and the sun starts to take its place, meeting in the middle with a gray light turning mauve. The three of us become a clock: the sun and moon ticking one direction over and behind me as I take steps forward on this round earth. The metric of a step, somehow more digestible than the unknown daunting miles between Fort Sumner and wherever I am on whatever road this is.

*

The sky pinks to brightness. I'm starting to feel worn from walking on little sleep, and there's a false feeling of having traveled further than I actually have since setting out in the dark. The shift in light creates a liminal landscape, the planet moving more rapidly and swiftly than me. The planet travels constantly without destination: perpetual orbit makes it a sort of vehicle, delivering whatever lives upon it to different planes of sky and light and time.

The planet gets to where it wants to be faster than I will. All I can do is move on top of it, wade through a landscape that has its own pace, as though we're on two conveyor belts moving at different speeds.

*

I stop to take a drink of water from the bottle in my pack. I don't have enough to last me the whole day. Maybe a car will stop. Maybe a gas station won't be too far off to make a detour. Maybe a desert oasis will emerge from a mirage.

Bonnie taught us a lot, but wilderness skills were lacking. Never taught us how to get water from a snake, for instance. There were a few weedy, flowering plants growing outside the house that she'd occasionally pluck, but I always thought she just liked the idea, the gesture of placing a flower in her mouth.

I settle my backpack over my shoulders again, the closest I get to being a snail. A sackful of objects to call home. Is a snail without its shell a slug or just homeless? ("A snail without its shell is most likely dead,"

I imagine Kit pointing out.) Transformed by the perception of being without.

Without shell, without Honda.

Without sister, without mother—Kit and I both in this particular boat at the moment. Our home in Silver River is without us. It was without Bonnie first. It got too quiet. The absence too loud, memories too many. So we packed up some jars, locked the door, and left. It felt better, immediately, to be held within the car, to be surrounded by the rumbling white noise of driving, to leave a feeling of helplessness in our wake.

*

Every once in a while someone passes—mostly semis and RVs, road beasts incapable of stopping for me, knowing I'd just slow them down.

*

Dragging of feet, weakness of quadriceps. Tiredness makes the brain swim in the skull, makes the horizon wobble. If I make it to that rock how far ahead I can't tell, I can curl up in its shadow (before the shadow is swept away by the noon sun). Catnap again, this time with clothes on, no circled wagons of Calamity Janes. Drowsy with heat again.

Feet kicking up rocks they can't bother to step over anymore. Veering further away from the road. The rock is getting bigger. Blinks are taking longer. I finally touch the rock and it is so warm, so surface full of tiny holes. I curl up in the shade, back against the rock, backpack under my head. Feet pointing toward the road. Pocketknife unfolded and gripped in my right hand. In case. Because, you never know. My eyes close and I notice the smell of piñon and scrub grass baking in the sun and then my mind drops into darkness.

Flits of dreams: Betty running into Mom's arms, Kit turning toward me in a laugh as the road whips by in the windows, the calf running down from heaven like an angel covered in legs and wings and flames, a coyote limping quickly down the road as the sound of a whining motor pours from its mouth.

Movement under my head, swift—I grip and throw my arm out before my eyes find the horizon line but I feel the blade make contact, see the pale boniness of an ankle between white jean cuff and white canvas shoe. Blood flashes out after a gasp from above—the ankle is within sight long enough for me to clock red droplets sinking into white and dust. My voice makes a noise and I flail as she kicks a flare of dirt in my face and I hear a cackle from this bandit in white as she runs back to an idling El Camino (also white under gypsum dust), a whip of red hair cyclonic in the wind. She tosses my limp backpack out the window as her driver takes off, engine going from whine to whinny as I scramble up. Adrenaline hasn't coordinated me out of sleep yet and my legs buckle under me.

My hand still holds the knife and my body is stunned even after I can't see the car anymore, can't hear it, the plume of dust that trailed behind it has fallen back to the ground. Not totally believing what just happened but sure as shit, there's my pack on the ground, spare clothes spewing out of it. I stand and walk toward it, picking up the socks and washcloth that were flung out together. The sandwich, with a coating of dust. I keep it anyway. The pack looks sad in the dirt, like roadkill. I dust it off and see what's left. No sewing kit. No small bundle of ones and fives. Shit. I look at the knife in my hand, the blood on the blade. Not a fair trade.

*

She left the water bottle but it leaked a little.

*

A series of sighs that crescendo into guttural moans from my animal throat.

*

What kind of lunatic asshole all-white desert cult did that person come from, anyway?

*

I breathe through my teeth until tears recede.

*

Body still intact, yes. Brain still working, check. Any idea what will happen now? The only thing to do is walk. I throw a rock, hard, on the road. It breaks, helps a little. Fantasize about somehow catching up with the El

Camino, slashing the tires, sugar in the gas tank (or darker yet—ashes), lying in wait in the backseat. Strangled to death with her own hair.

Except I don't think prey animals get even. Is that what I am—a prey animal? Vulnerable, separated from my herd. Hunted, unbeknownst to me. To my thief, I could have been anyone, most likely. I was only an easy target because I was alone and asleep. I hope. I guess it's possible that they'd seen me—or us—somewhere on the road before, maybe saw money change hands, maybe'd been tailing me even after Betty picked me up, maybe—maybe paranoia is another prey animal trait. I remember a cluster of antelope grazing on our back field one day, how they stood so still when listening and walked so delicately and deliberately. Never had all their heads down at once. Then the next morning they were gone, and there was an antelope-sized broken ring of fur on the grass, a fading drag of blood.

What would Kit do: probably count it as a loss for the rest of her life, revenge tucked away in the back of her mind. Quickly calculate how this might impact the rest of this journey and go from there, trying to make up for it.

What would Bonnie do: make sure her beehive was still in place, tsk about how the thief must have been desperate or deranged, and toss a handful of dirt over her shoulder to mark the past being behind her.

I scoop up some dirt, throw it over my shoulder right as the wind blows against my back. Take a deep breath and decide to watch out for El Caminos and people dressed in all white. I put my backpack on and snug the straps tighter, stretch tall with my arms overhead. Thinking of antelope, I lope on.

*

I picture the box of Saltines, the bag of bread and jar of peanut butter all jostling behind the driver's seat in the Honda. Another oversight.

*

A reckoning with my choice to separate, to be alone. This is what I wanted, but only as a means—my aim at the start seemed strong enough to take me the entire way, but now in the reality of this journey, it's flagging. The desire is still there—the image of the calf becoming dustier by the minute, her glass eyes boring holes through the walls of the museum and down the highway, her body containing both mystery and answer too powerful for a jar and therefore deserving liberation from the case she's been in for decades.

On top of that, a feeling of kinship. Imagining her herd from above, where her anomaly might not be so obvious, lost in the legs and bony backs of other cows: this is how the three of us—Bonnie, Kit, and me—had blended in with our community, such as it was. Not living close to neighbors afforded everyone some privacy, and at school or at the store, rumors remained rumors. Bonnie didn't tell us much about her own childhood, but we knew her family'd been shamed out of a few towns and when she set out on her own, she drifted around until she finally felt that New Mexico could be called *home*. We seem to have inherited this drifting, this appetite for movement. Other things inherited from down the line: a dimple on the left, always sneezing twice, ability to keep a secret immaculately safe.

We weren't raised to be ashamed of the family or our shared gift for sensing and capturing, but Bonnie seemed to have a sense for knowing better than to flaunt it. We didn't advertise or sell in town. If a neighbor knew to come to her, they did so with respect, with reverence (or perhaps fear). Unlike the calf, our differences were hidden on the inside, borne in the blood. I wonder if that had helped us survive longer. Someone told me once that love is when you wonder what a person does when they're apart from you. How much of love is curiosity, then?

Reuniting—with the calf and Kit—is down the road, waiting. At the present, I'm with myself. A choice made twice, really: first peeling off from Kit, and then leaving Betty. And what will I do when night comes? Instinct says keep the blood moving, keep the eyes open, and walk all night if I can.

*

Footstep sounds interrupted by stomach growls. The predator inside, demanding to feed. I haven't seen a sign yet—either I haven't gotten very far or there really is nothing out here. I feel that yearning ache in the jaw of wanting to chew, to sink teeth into something. I think I would lick the inside of a to-go container someone pitched out their window, but the only discarded things on either side of the road are rust and rubber, and even those are rare. I'm not quite having cartoon hallucinations of bushes turning into burgers, but close. I think about what the antelopes may have been eating outside our house, if any of it was the same as what Bonnie'd picked. What vegetation there was was sparse and scraggly limbed. Remember the little blue starbursts of chicory that opened to the sun. Remember learning in school that the roots were a coffee substitute, that chicory belonged to the daisy family. Picture a family of daises. Add it to the mental list of things to watch for.

*

It's windy but the sun has nothing to hide behind. The skin on my shoulders is pink; I wonder if it will blister later, if I will cook so well. I carry my pack over my head until the sun ticks further behind me, until my arms ache, until it seems pointless.

I wonder if heat intensifies hunger more than cold does. When your body screams with heat, are you more likely to have deeper pangs of hunger than when your body trembles with cold? Who was cannibalism more prevalent with—pioneers coming west in the summer or arctic explorers?

And here I am without anyone to cannibalize except myself, were I driven to it. No money for food, nowhere to buy it from; no jars to sell for money, no one to sell them to. I stop and take the sad sandwich from my backpack. The wax paper is torn, some peanut butter has squished out of the bread, and there's a good amount of dirt that can't be brushed off. Knowing the sandwich is a recipe for thirst, I bite into it, practically feel the enzymes in my spit start to break it down and absorb it. I eat as slow as my hunger will let me. The dirt adds some bitterness, a little acrid, but like the sandwich at the gas station, I think of consuming land, a dirt that I earned. Maybe that will make it more filling. I swallow the last bite of crust, lick the smears of peanut butter from the paper, fold it into a small square and tuck it back in my pack. Then it's as if the sandwich never existed; I may have only reminded myself of what eating is: two bites forward, one bite back.

*

I walk through blazing gold that softens as the sky returns to pink. Irritating loops of scarcely remembered songs cycle through my mind in an effort toward preoccupation. Every once in a while, a car goes by in either direction, but no one slows and I make no move to hitch. There's a weight in me to move by myself, just these legs for this leg, anyway. I know it's partly due to cultivating independence and trying out desire as propulsion, but it is also fear of being alone that is keeping me alone. All this walking, all this horizon surrounding me—a new sort of isolation. Without a clear, certain end in sight. Find myself feeling raw and strange, like the ragged pulp and edge of a melon broken by dropping. Exposed, but to my own self only. I do not want to share this with anyone.

*

Shadows are dissolving as the light dims and blues, turning the ground and rocks and grass and me into nearly the same color, quicker than I can register.

Unexpectedly as ever, the overwhelm of *I miss her* heaves over me like a wave.

What a good time to be feeling a heartache like this.

This longing for home, for a familiarity, it's an unexpected and specific slice of grief.

Will it stick or will it slip? The bulk of grief, I learned after Bonnie, was feeling intensely uncomfortable in the body, in the mind, in time. A desperation to not *be* anywhere or anything until it was over, without being able to fully articulate what the *it* was, while being too paralyzed to do anything but quake under the weight of this impossible, irreparable rift. To only suffer in the eclipse of Before and After. To only ache.

And here we are again (or still), a little bit. Brought on by this isolation, the ripping away from Kit, leaving the camaraderie of Betty, the stun of highway robbery. Stirred an ache. The ache this time feels too difficult to move. Just like this morning, can't walk around it.

So far my feet are still lifting and setting down, still finding the edge of the road in the milky moonlight. Blood still pumping. Stars out from hiding, plane lights blinking between them in their own trajectories. I almost laugh thinking of how no one knows where I am right now—not because it's funny, but because it is absurd. The absurdity of being as tiny and flung-out as one of these stars. Wandering in the desert, as people have done for eons. Am I wandering if I'm following the road? At the edge of disappearing. Drifting off into the dark.

Do I dare risk sleeping roadside again? Made even more vulnerable by the dark, the darkness that leads to seeing flashes of the backs of your own eyes, pupils dilated as much as they can, like small animals unto themselves, trying to be aware, to protect. Every body part and system its own entity, fingers crossed they work together. Feeling the tug of muscle memory from before—striking out with the knife, like a snake—proof that the body's cohesion has worked fairly well before, and recently.

"My dogs are barkin'," Bonnie would say after spending all day on her feet.

Silent and blunt as hooves, mine.

A car passes, brights on, and illuminates the edge of a ditch just ahead and to the right. This opens What Ifs, and if I were sleeping I'd at least be staying put, rather than putting myself in the danger of what I might blindly walk into. It feels the way this morning did. But with an ache. I just want something to lean against. Something that will stay.

At the same time: a fear of stopping. A feeling that, were I to stop moving, to halt pursuit, the current of time would continue to flow around me but not through me. That if I allowed myself to become a person who pauses, I would cease moving forward—not that I then wouldn't wake up tomorrow and continue to put one foot in front of the other, but that a certain light or fire would go out, coals unstoked and dying, no longer powering my engine.

So I continue moving forward, slowly, with careful feet like paws feeling out a step before fully taking it. My arms out in front a bit, like antennae or whiskers. I fall in line with my own slow rhythm, sometimes stumbling, in this desert shuffle like a new dance.

*

The quietness of this invisibility washes through my brain and it occurs to me to capture—or try to capture—this ache of isolation. An urge from the inside to use the moves I already know.

MISSING INVENTORY: a jar or vessel. I shuffle further off the road, settle on my knees, begin pawing at the dirt like an animal trying to find something it intended to save for later. My fingers feel too soft for the soil, packed by feet and tires and time, but a couple inches down, a couple inches across feels sufficient. The void is a hollow black, surrounded by moonlight.

How do you coax out something already present inside of you? It occurs to me this may be bordering on exorcism, but this feeling isn't possessive or demonic, just something I would like to have out of me. A snake sheds its skin when it's ready and maybe this is another method, a practice of detaching.

Capturing at night has always felt harder; time feels like it stops more heavily. Less of a gauge for what's happening, where something is coming from.

I kneel with my fingers in the hole, palms up. I focus on the ache, the feeling it puts in my chest, a gnawing open, a faint pulling away. Loss and loneliness. A *how did we get here?* confusion, life swept away; the melodrama has me picturing the words "bereft" and "unmoored" which feel true, and they're big—the whole feeling seems bigger than me and something of me shakes out from under it—a vision of myself repeatedly undulating out from under a vast, floppy cloud until I feel funneling in my fingers, a pull of gravity down into this shallow hole and my left hand sweeps the loose dirt over my right fingers, and then I pull my right hand free, push more dirt over the void and I wonder if it worked.

*

My bones feel heavy. I start walking. Not sure that whole cloud, that whole feeling, could fit in the space I made. But if some of it is kept in there and no longer in me, well, at least there's that. At least I tried. Bonnie, I tried.

I walk as daylight rises and eventually there's what looks like a fork in the road, but the part that turns right goes from pavement to gravel and cuts between a line of tall dark trees and a yard of brambly grass and bushes and my eye that had been kept out for it lights upon a chicory bush. I walk toward it, wondering what it will taste like, feeling hunger in my fingers, and I see a small adobe house behind a scrap wood fence. I realize my fingers are gripping an arm of chicory when a woman with braids of gray hair and faded overalls springs up and then back down without looking up. The chicory belongs to someone. I walk closer and see she's in a garden plot. She seems calm and focused, energy flowing between her body and the earth. I put my hands on the fence, just above my waist. I clear my throat. "Excuse me," I say.

She looks up, unstartled, hands still digging and troweling. "Hi there. Saw you pause at the road. Wondered if you'd come down this way."

"I didn't know anyone lived out here," as if I know where exactly I am, and immediately regret saying this because of course people live out here, same as how Kit and I lived in such a flung-away place.

"Sure do, just plenty of room between us." She looks up at me and smiles like the sun.

"What are you growing?"

She grabs a tall green tail rising out of the ground and pulls. Purple and caked in moist soil, a heart is freed. "Beets," she says. She beams at her prize, then drops it on top of a heap of others in a basket.

"I'm Gloria," I say.

"Rosemary," she says. Rubs her chin with the back of her hand. She cocks her head. "Was there something you needed help with, Gloria?"

I swallow. "You have chicory in your yard," I gesture behind me, "and um—do you think I could have some?"

She squints at me. "Well sure, but if you don't mind my asking, what d'ya need it for?"

Embarrassment of hunger. "I just haven't eaten in a while and I know it's edible, and I'm not sure when my next burrito will be." I shake out a nervous laugh.

Rosemary says, "Ah," then carefully pulls out another beet. "Tell ya what, Glor', I don't have a burrito but I certainly have more than enough provisions to spare. Let me finish this row and you can come inside. No need to waste your time gnawing chicory. Unless that's really what you have a craving for?"

My face, flushed with heat. "That sounds much better, if it's no trouble, I really wasn't trying to—"

"I know. And that's why."

I thumb a splinter in the fence. "To tell you the truth, I can't say I'd really know which part of the chicory plant to eat."

She laughs gently which I think means she isn't surprised.

I watch her hands sink into the ground, fingers knowing what to feel for, like a midwife assisting a birth.

"Do you, um. Do you wonder much about how they look while they're hidden underground? What form they take on and how it changes, I mean."

"Oh, constantly." She springs up and then drops a few feet down the row again. "That hidden metamorphosis—" she pulls "—from seed to fruit—fascinating process." She frees another beet.

*

Inside, the kitchen is warm wood and tile, leaves of all different shapes jetting out of various pots and pitchers, vines trailing down into the enamel sink. It feels well-loved and tended-to. Rosemary starts rinsing off beets in the sink, tells me to sit at the table. Dalmatian salt and pepper shakers stand on a palm-sized crocheted doily. The table is marked with little dents from the ends of silverware and rings from sweaty glasses, an archive of people gathering and eating here. Again I feel a twinge of shame at my appetite—it's not her responsibility to feed me, a stranger—it's no one's but my own—and then there's the problem of overeating your welcome. But she offered, so I'll do my best to accept it.

She takes a jar down from over the stove. Her movements are slow and thoughtful, like she only exists in this moment. She holds the jar up in the light coming through the window: the sun filters through the red and fuchsia wedges inside, playing through the translucencies, casting smudges and stains of red light on her arms and face, on my hands on the table. It's lovely. I want to live in it, inside that warm, red, watery light, in this kitchen trapped in amber still syrupy.

She pops open the jar and spoons a few of the beet pieces into a small bowl, places it in front of me with a fork, pours me a glass of water. "First course," she says as she sits down across from me with a cutting board, paring knife, and a bowl of damp beets. I spear a wedge and in my mouth it's surprisingly sweet, and tangy with vinegar.

"The flavor—there's so much," I say.

"It was a good crop that year, lots of lightning storms." She takes a beet in one hand and starts working the flat blade just under the skin of it. "So. You're between burritos."

I look down at the table and my hand on the bowl. I think about the version of this introductory conversation I'd had with Betty, think about what was stolen from me, think about the feeling I trapped and buried last night.

"My sister and I have been driving—well, we split, just for now." I push the words out. "Our—our mom died. Last year. And we needed to, you know, come up for air. So we've been traveling. And now I—no, *we* are in pursuit of different things. We had to head in different directions. Didn't really bring enough food with me."

"How long've you been on the road?" she asks softly.

"I'm not sure. Maybe just a couple days, on my own. My sister—it's temporary." I place another piece of beet in my mouth.

"Before I left home," she says, pushing peelings to one corner of the board, her hands painted with pink, "my mother told me not to bother with worry, to just show up hungry and let the rest sort itself out. So far, she's been right. Plus, I think the hunger can propel you—that's what I told my daughter, too."

I remember belonging to someone like a daughter. I remember hearing Bonnie say "my daughter," just like that.

My mouth caves over the beet, face contracting too fast for me to react and then the room is swimming in tears. I manage to swallow and bring my hands to my face. (If in a jar: SHAME OF TENDERNESS.) Heat from my sobs clouds between my face and my hands.

"I'm sorry." My voice sounds unfamiliar, squeaking. Rosemary moves around the table and puts an arm around me, rubs my back; I heave with sobs as big as the untethered feeling inside me. I have only an idea of where I am on the map, in this desert, but I feel lost at sea, just a tiny boat bobbing up and down, only in control of which direction I'm pointed. I guess I hadn't captured that entire aching feeling, or it found a way to follow me.

She pauses, grabs a beet from her bowl. "This beet is a root," Rosemary says, waving it toward me by the green. "It was buried solid underground, in the dark, formed by the fate of the seed interacting with the elements of the universe. And this root, this beet, did what it set out to do, got along fine, and then I came along and dug it up, which has likely scared the hell out of it, right?" She sets it on the cutting board and poises the knife over it. "But now that it's been unearthed, excavated—" thwack "—everything that's been growing inside gets to show up."

Deep magenta seeps on the board, concentric circles show ghostly in the dense flesh. For a split second I think of Bonnie, all the deep red I couldn't help imagining spreading on the diner's checkered floor.

Rosemary brings the section of beet to her mouth, bites in and sucks it like an orange. It leaves her lips bright pink, her teeth stained and outlined in red. Her smile is painted with this makeshift gore, and if I weren't convinced of her kindness I would probably be terrified. Maybe it's because I'm desperate. Maybe it's because my instinct says I can trust her.

*

She shares more food with me—refried beans and rice; a homemade tamale from deep within the freezer; an egg, fried, salted and peppered, reclining on a generous slab of buttered sourdough. She sits with me the whole time.

"So, where'd your daughter leave home for?" I ask between bites.

"Well, she was planning on going to school in California, but she was killed in a horse-riding accident summer before she would've started. That was about five years ago."

I swallow hard. "I'm so sorry." I can't think of what to say so I say it again. "I'm so sorry. What was her name?"

"Angelica Jane. Everyone called her AJ." She rolls a stray grain of rice between her fingers and half smiles. "The horse we called the Day-Mare. She's out back."

I set down my fork. "She's—You kept the horse?"

"Well, it wasn't her fault. Turned out she had been going blind more rapidly than we realized and on this last ride, she got spooked pretty bad—AJ got bucked, and the horse ran home."

I think of when I got the surprise of Bonnie's death—disbelief, my brain not comprehending the information, the horrible impulse of imagination that manifests a body sprawled without life.

"AJ loved that horse, wouldn't've wanted me to put her down or sell her. She loved her like an extension of herself."

"And the horse is totally blind now?"

"Her eyes had gotten infected, so…the vet did what they do to horses with infected, blind eyes." She takes the loaf of bread and, in the cut-away face of it, gouges two holes with her thumbs.

*

69

Rosemary pushes her generosity further and lets me take a shower, lays out some blankets and a pillow on her couch for me. The relief is nearly unbearable, to be washed and clean and ungrimed, I can't remember how long ago the last motel night was. The room is various shades of earth, the adobe walls undulating up into the ceiling. The brown leather sofa faces a sliding glass door that opens to an adobe patio and a tall garden. The blanket is strewn with short white hairs, but I don't see a dog or cat so I don't ask. The daylight comes in cool and pale. I hear the soft ripping noises of Rosemary pulling weeds and vegetables from the front garden. As soon as I lie down, I realize I'm more tired than when I lay down next to the fateful boulder. But feeling so sure and secure and tended-to; feeling mothered.

I wake up hours later in the afternoon. The light has changed and the air is warmer. The room is still and I didn't dream. My eyes open to catch a glimpse through the sliding door: dark brown with some silver dapple, a huff of exhalation. My blood quickens. I go out to the yard, sprawling with wildflowers waving their heads on thin, curving stems. The black tail swishes at a fly. Head dips down to the grass. Haunches twitch. I feel slightly levitated, gazing upon this giant. She raises her head and I wonder if I've made a mistake in approaching from behind, even staying several feet away. I make a wide circle so I can see her from the front.

I behold the face of the Day-Mare. Where there were eyes, there are two smooth hollows, lovingly crafted, not a bit of crude scarring. As if eyes had never been there at all. What moves underneath, behind the hollows? What does that part of the brain reach out for? I feel regarded by these blank pits.

I step closer and slowly raise my hand and the horse leans forward to sniff. Thick lips move against my palm. I angle my hand to the side of her mouth and she moves forward and down, head-to-hand affection. She feels familiar; she feels like she thinks I'm familiar. The eye pits are level with my eyeballs and I move my hand further up, slowly feel the ridge of one socket with my thumb, then dip into the velvet orbit. The skin feels stretched against a delicate emptiness, like there's just a slight gap between the skin and what matter has filled in behind it. I consider the size of the cavity, the size her sight had been, what long eyelashes and careful lids had once been here. Both my hands are alongside her face, petting from socket to jaw to ear. I trust that the Day-Mare would move away if it weren't wanted, or that she would find a language to tell me not to touch.

The light bounces up to the underside of her left socket, illuminating the hole, glimmers of an oil puddle in the arcing hairs. Glows a bit, as if lit from within. As if a memory of sight is refracting its way out. I trace the thin grain of hairs, brown and silver, flowing in one direction like a field of tall grass in strong wind. My fingers explore the cranial space and I wonder what happens between the eyes of a horse when the eyes are no more.

I'm sure she can smell that I'm not AJ. But I wonder if I remind her. I wonder if I remind Rosemary. I take my hands from her face and move to hug her neck, rest the side of my face against the mane, listen to the air and blood moving through her body, the small clicks and gurgles that a body makes by being alive. I run my fingers through her dark mane, wonder how AJ must've threaded her fingers through the same, out of love, out of fear.

And then, that sense of being tapped on a third shoulder, of something existing beyond this body. I stay very still, and wait to see if it stays.

The breeze moves the branches of the small oak tree, and it stays.

The sun bakes perfume out of the herbs and flowers and dirt, and it stays.

I hear Rosemary go inside and set down her heavy basket, and it stays.

I slip away from the horse and go back in the house. I grab the jar, now empty of beets, drying by the sink. I lock eyes with Rosemary but don't say anything. I grab the lid too.

I retrace my steps to the horse, sidle up like I'm slipping back under a blanket. It stayed. I feel Rosemary watching from the kitchen window. I hold the jar in the air near the Day-Mare, I close my eyes and breathe in the feeling, I breathe it out. I feel her heartbeat like my own. Something stirs and flutters, then a feeling like a mechanism, one piece spinning within another piece, spinning in the opposite direction. A special kind of vertigo. I can't feel the boundary between my hand and the jar, between my cheek and her neck.

Something swirls, coming in in all directions, and then the galloping, shining horizon moving past both sides of a face, all four hooves off the ground at one instant, the thundering of the body against land, patches of light reflecting and refracting, shimmers and specters and then everything bright.

THE DAY-MARE'S LAST SIGHT.

It's okay, I think to the invisible, *you can get in if you want to.* Just a coaxing. The air hesitates, then sinks into the jar.

I screw the lid on, lean my head against the horse's neck, and say thank you.

I turn around. Rosemary's stepped out into the yard, into the sun. Her arms are folded in front of her chest.

"She's a gentle creature," she says when I get near.

"She is." I lift the jar in front of my chest and draw in a breath. "Did you notice anything just now?"

"Well, you were so still it seemed like time stopped for a bit, and I thought maybe you were sleepwalking. I did notice she seemed completely relaxed while you stood next to her. Like she was resting her senses."

Where to begin? Another deep breath. "This is what my sister and I do," I gesture with the jar. "It's what our mother taught us to do, and what her mother taught her to do, all the way back. We sense invisibilities—energies, spirits, whatever you want to call it—and capture them, if they want to be caught."

"She taught you how to sense them?"

I dig my toes into the warm earth. "There's a lot of waiting involved. A lot of following hunches." I think of her garden. "Sometimes I think of it as a feeling similar to believing something huge once started out as something so tiny—that tree, or that horse—without seeing it happen. Or all the things in the atmosphere that we can't see but breathe in anyway." What would Kit's spiel be? "I'm sorry I don't really know how to explain it better. It's almost like it passes through us, over us, like a conductor. Something that's just *there*, and then we wait for it to be in *here*." I gesture with the jar.

She gives me the same amused and knowing look she did when I asked for chicory. "Not that different from planting a seed, waiting. I believe it."

I hand her the jar and say, "It's time I got going, and I can't thank you enough—for everything—and you should have this. I think it's the Day-Mare's last memory of sight. Maybe AJ's last—"

She says "Oh" like air being rolled from her lungs. She takes the jar, looks in at the clear contents, holds it with both hands like something precious. I wonder if it's a fair trade.

*

Outside her front door, I snug my laces and straighten my pack, familiar on my shoulders. I ask Rosemary one last question: "How far to Fort Sumner?"

She says, "About five miles," and points down the road in the direction I was headed this morning.

*

The road into Fort Sumner is long and green, sloping slowly over the distance. The earth rises up gray miles away on either side of me. Walking feels good now. My body knows what's up. Lungs syncopated with legs, all joints moving loose and easy. I can't see the bend in the road toward the calf yet but I feel the pull of it.

*

It rains. The sky rolls darker and the water bounces off the ground, bounces off my skin. I can feel every rock through my thin-soled shoes, tiny fists pushing me forward. It hails. It hails me. Hear Kit's voice saying, *Little sister, the sky is falling.* I walk with my backpack shielding my head. The ice is about the size and weight of garbanzo beans. Just as quickly, the sky dries again.

*

I walk myself out of energy. The body feels heavy and unrelated to me, so I call it *the body.* The body is, at this point, just something my brain totes around, to tote my brain around. The journey wears out the body and the body continues moving forward. The brain clings to the notion of the end, of victory, of plans working out, of two halves meeting. It's enough to propel.

*

A co-op appears off the side of the road. To make sure it's not a mirage, I go in, grab an avocado and a stale roll from a dark pastry case. The woman behind the counter might be dead except she's sipping on the cigarette in her mouth. She has a snarl of blonde hair and we don't say a word to each other. I look her in the eye as I count out coins from the leave-a-penny-take-a-penny tray, a brazen move, but the fact that the tray is there at all with coins in it is sign enough. *See how they treat you.* A quarter, three dimes, three nickels, and twenty-nine pennies. Dinner.

On the step outside, I cut into the fruit with my pocketknife, which no longer bears traces of blood. I remember Bonnie telling me, as she rotated her blade around one, avocados were also called alligator pears—a peel of ancient armor protecting tender greeny-yellow flesh. Alternating between scooping out the soft green fat with the tip of my knife and tearing off a dry hunk of bread with my teeth. Crumb and squish. A desert meal. No one around to disturb me. The water in my pack is warm from body and sun. My mind is as wide as the landscape and full of the rushing sounds of wind, traveling particles from one state to the next.

Here is a sound of whipping wind: ubububububububububub-vubvubvubvubvubvubub and some pitch inside it found the memory in me of my ear pressed to Bonnie's chest. Thank you wind, thank you memory.

*

The gas station shop is packed with CDs, cases bearing names completely foreign to me, and taxidermied heads—deer, rams, hares, jackalope, a bull elk—all mounted on lacquered wooden plaques and hanging near the ceiling.

Interesting how you never see the heads of horses or cows fixed and mounted like this. I know if the calf was just a head I'd feel different. Less inclined.

I find two dimes deep in that tiny, forgettable pocket, which affords me two postcards, *Greetings from the Land of Enchantment!* No stamps.

> DEAR B— You were so reliable. I mean, when Kit would move on without me, frequently, frustratedly, her being the older daughter, you did your best to quell any loneliness that may have welled up. Funny, the image of welling—water seeping up from the ground. In such a dry place like this, that is what you were to me. That was how I needed you. To keep the ground of me from cracking and breaking and blowing away. I miss you. I feel I maybe am starting to blow away. Maybe Kit has left me behind for good this time. —G

> DEAR K— When did I start feeling you would leave me behind? I wonder if, since B died, I've pinned more dependence on you, whether or not you want it. I'm not sure we ever learned how to balance it (never had to, like this). Maybe I'm worried I'm the one leaving. I miss you. I hope you come back. When did we split? We used to practically read each other's minds. Then a fork in the road

and who knows how many hundreds of miles later. This won't reach you but I hope I do. —G

INVENTORY OF MAILBOX: thought-feelings for safe keeping.

*

On invisible things: our market would be bigger if the container wasn't the only tangible part of the deal. If there was some taxidermied evidence or a bared bone for show, it would be some sort of signifier—that we had touched some part of the animals we make claims on. But not everything we gather comes from a tangible source. The object isn't the thing, anyway.

*

A billboard in the distance gets closer and closer, all it says is EAT with an arrow pointing west and the EAT just gets bigger and bigger. It yells at me by the time I pass it, after I realize I have no more food with me. But I don't worry.

*

The road finally bends. Bleached wood and brick buildings line the wide street, and I walk right up. I sit on the slope of grass at the edge of the parking lot on the west side of the Billy the Kid Museum, waiting. The engine ticks out heat under the hood of a white Ford SUV, shiny and new-looking, the kind that you know is probably secretly designed to look like a woman's hips. Little black wing stuck to the grill, half the flight of a bat, clutching onto the thin bars of metal. Had I a jar, I might try to capture this lost flight, whatever message it might hold. But being jarless, I just sit with it. I can feel it in the bat body—what it takes for the entire body to flap, the navigation informed by messages bouncing off your face, the calm induced by hanging upside down. I think of how some bats are domestically cute, others have wrinkly wads of faces. Either way the face is designed to more safely and effectively transport them through the sky and thus through time with evolution. You can be ugly and still move forward and anyway it's subjective and anyway even the cute can carry rabies.

I start thinking of what Kit may or may not have captured in the ghost town. I never saw what label she put on the jar. An infinite number of possibilities could've been flying, floating around that place, and who knows what could've been attracted to the white dress she put on. I wonder if that was her reason—flashier bait on the hook. A wolf in something like sheep's clothing. Is the trick of it the part I don't like?

My thoughts begin teetering on the danger of it all being a sort of scam where I fooled myself into believing anything was happening, that I was achieving anything. This weird crisis of some sort of faith, this being unable to raise something from the dead and wondering if anything had ever been raised or captured by me, by her, by Bonnie, at all. I know what it looked like when they did it, how it seemed to work for them. A quantifiable skill like setting a snare, lying in wait. The delicate task of trapping something autonomous but not necessarily unsuspecting. Why is it so easy for me to lean toward this, even after the Day-Mare, the shallow grave for isolation ache, the emanations from the bat just now? Why do I feel like when I do it, it's smaller, quieter, it's *less*? Kit has always been more adept at the practice, but there was no competition growing up, Bonnie didn't allow that—I remember one instance of "Look what I got! Gloria's is empty," but that bud was nipped before it was fully out of Kit's mouth. "It's just that there are no differences," she'd said, "You feel the way you feel and they come to you the way they choose to come to you. You can't control either side of it—might take a while to learn that." To learn it, let alone just remember it, I suppose. To also remember to trust the hunch, the feeling that something to capture may be there—to trust the invisibility itself.

The calf is dead, gutted and stuffed. She is already trapped, probably now a different soul altogether, or at least something liminal. She's stuffed and stuck, ergo there was no deception involved—nothing to doubt. A stationary object. Is it so black and white? So immediate a transition?

On the contrary, I'm taking her back out into the world, a liberation away from rusted machinery and homage to the long-dead, long-ugly, outlaw Billy boy.

Is it right? Is it *more* right? Is this really love? It's like finding an amputated limb of my own flesh and insisting it will reattach and work again if I carry it around long enough. If I hold her close enough.

*

Two older women—matching white bowl cuts and khaki shorts—walk out of the museum and head toward me.

"I coulda sworn it was real, Peg," says the one.

"I've been telling you for twenty years, there's no way it's the real anything. And I—was—right—!" says the other.

"But it's *his* museum, for chrissakes!" says the one, raising her hands in exasperation. They split when they get to the SUV I'm seated next to, Peg heading for the driver's seat. I look at her face and she rolls her eyes at me, mocking in confidentiality.

"Most of that stuff in there, the guns and buggies and tools—not his," she says across the windshield. "You think they moved not only a jail cell he'd spent a few nights in but also his got-damn *grave* to this rinky-dink museum?"

The other one makes a sound of embarrassed defeat and gets in the truck. As Peg opens her door I ask if she knows what time it is.

"Quarter till five," she says.

"Just a few hours of daylight left!" says the other one, her voice muffled behind the windshield. "C'mon, Peg!"

Peg winks at me, waves half-handedly as she backs out of her parking spot. I wave at them, at the bat in their grill, wishing good luck to it and to all the tiny creatures that hitched a ride on its body.

*

Thinking on thievery. A band of thieves. I remember Bonnie explaining to us about our ancestry, past generations constructing their lives out in southwestern desert, lonely-seeming lives of hard work, independence, struggle. Certain crones pushed to the side, where they found something like magic—ways of communicating with the earth and the lives that had come before them—and because this looked strange and unnatural and insane to most people, they were pushed aside even more. Bonnie said that was just fine since things were richer at the sides anyway, where they hadn't been trod bare by everyone else.

I picture women holding their hands out to be filled by the electric air, by other powers and lingering souls that had also been discarded by mankind. Practices that were less and less welcomed as civilization crowded in.

Bonnie'd also pointed out that there were those who were outlaws. Runaways, bandits, and horse thieves. I wonder if liberation was part of their motivation, too, wondered what they were concerned with getting freed. If this was a legacy that was meant to be passed down and what they would think of me thieving this long-dead and deformed calf, no ill intentions, not driven by greed or cruelty. I can imagine them scoffing, but I prefer to imagine them cheering. I like to imagine they welcome me as one of them, recognize their blood in my veins.

How many of these ancestors were also sisters? How many grew up together, feeling the same as one another, lives alongside each other? Splitting off eventually and expanding the family like tree roots, propagation or not, lives running parallel yet so different—inherently an alternate version of yourself, the life you could have had, if—if—if—.

Of course identity is tied up in Kit. We could have been each other. From far away we look the same. Like stars. Like fleas. And just like stars and fleas, I realize we are surrounded by infinite space allowing us to be vastly different, too.

*

Once the cars are gone and the daylight has faded enough, I get on my feet and slowly circle the building. A breeze kicks up and I breathe in big. No cameras. But passing a west side window, there's a light on over the counter of the gift shop—a younger girl, high-school aged, is finishing up her day's work. She looks more at ease than Kimberley at the gas station, who had no company but her thoughts on her sparring angels. I sink down a bit and watch—a thin stack of cash shoved into the bank bag, the day's receipts clipped to the bookkeeping ledger. I wonder if she likes the responsibility, if she has a plan for if someone worse than me were to steal away things with more worldly value than the calf, if she'd be afraid or if she'd react with swift conviction that she was the one in charge. As if she hears me thinking, she looks around, looks over at the window. I hope the sun's set enough that I don't look like anything. I blink and she's gone away from the counter. A second later she walks back, a denim purse slung over her shoulder; she pushes through the front door and double checks it's locked behind her. I press my back against the side of the building, flakes of bumpy paint pressing against my skin. Footsteps. She appears around the corner, eyes wide as she sees me, one hand frozen in her purse, groping for car keys.

"Hey?" She says, voice more confused than scared.

"Uh…y'all are closed for the day?" I blurt.

"Yeah," she says, still frozen. "Just locked up."

I try to relax my body, slide into a more casual stance. "Guess I'll… come back tomorrow, then?" Will she expect me? Will she remember my face from these shadows?

"Okay." She starts to step back, step around me, give me a wide berth in case I pounce, a reaction I am familiar with but didn't mean to evoke, not wanting to encounter any reaction at all. My movements start to reflect hers and I back up as well so we can take off in opposite directions, but we don't turn our backs on each other.

"I wasn't—I'm not a—" stammering, I don't know what to tell her to get her to not worry about me, to not be led by her concern to call the police or whatever sheriff protects this town. Even in the dark (or especially in the dark), I probably look like the vagrant I more or less am these days. We're several feet apart now. "Do you know where the nearest bus stop is?" Do they have busses that go through here? Make her think I'm just browsing, passing through, on my way to leaving.

"No," she says, stepping back to the driver's side door of a gray Chevy. "I don't." Then, maybe thinking I'm about to ask for a ride, she gets in the car quick, starts the engine and sits with the headlights on. The beams don't hit me and I take off in a diagonal between her car and the museum, over the grass slope I'd been sitting on for hours just before, across the next parking lot and around the high brick building until I've made a wide enough arc that I can see her finally pull out and head down the road, away from me, away from the museum.

I feel sick at the thought of someone in a uniform coming to patrol, to check if I'm still prowling. I feel sicker that I put that girl in that position, of surprise at finding someone where they're not supposed to be, when they're not supposed to be there, where they're not expected. The shift in expectations when the problem of an entire person wedges themselves in. I sink down against the building, knees by my ears and hidden (I hope) by a trashcan that says PUT 'ER THERE! on the side and I say, "I know, I put her there, I put me there," and I remember what I was doing before I put 'er there, waiting for the right time to get the calf. And then I think it's now or never. If someone with a gun and a badge is on the way, then I need to act fast—no one's pulled into the museum lot yet—and then my legs are sprinting across one lot to the next, feet barely touching the ground but so sure of themselves. I don't feel myself think; I only *do*. The weak spot in the building's design—the small courtyard-type area, open-air, enclosed by a thick brick wall. Nothing to boost myself up with, no way I can scale it on my own. Around the backside of the museum, I look for anything I can use—no boxes or pallets, absolutely nothing ladder-like, but, oh! an old paint bucket, now half-full of cigarette ends and ashes and it will have to do. I haul it by the wall, step up on it, and I can almost reach, stretch a little more, sweaty palms grasping the edge, one shoe's rubber gaining a little traction against the wall, one wild grip in my muscles (all of them!), and I find the leverage; the paint can spills over under my toes, my ribcage is hauled over the top, swing of a leg and for a second I straddle the wall. I dare to pause. Everything is still—the museum, the parking lot, the street—and I see it all from above. No lights have come on, no cars screech into the lot, no sirens in the distance. Swing the other leg and drop down. The sound of my weight on the gravel. With freedom on the brain, I walk through the courtyard, hearing only the crunch of my shoes on sand, the thrum of outlaw blood in my heart. The machinery, the rusted sculpture, the fake graves of Billy the Kid and his compadre—all reduced to dark shapes. I walk past Billy the Kid's jail-cell door, walk past the sign telling me it's not the real thing. *The real thing.* I head toward the real thing: toward you. The door to the inside is wooden, and, at the risk of fingerprints, I turn the knob. It's loose, but locked. Remembering Kit getting her way into the house in the ghost town, I encourage its opening, and with a groan and a crack, the lock obliges. I'm not aware of removing or breaking any glass. One minute it's around you on five sides and the next minute we're breathing the same air and I see my hands reaching for you, your form phosphorescent. You feel dry like the landscape had been trying to tell me about you. Sawdust leaking from small seams and I say, *I know, I know, shh.* I take you away from this fortress of manmade objects and manmade information and bring you out under the stars and you haven't seen them for so long I'm sure we're both weeping. Different substances but the body expressing, nonetheless. In the morning they'll find the trail you leak behind us, follow it through two rooms and outside, right over the wall, and then going out to the road in front of the museum, abruptly stopping in a dusty puddle of awkward maneuvers when I settle you into the backseat of the Honda, our getaway car, our driver of course the triumphantly returned Sister Kit and the engine quietly purrs because it's glad to see us and glad to be taking us away.

PART III

INVENTORY: one beautiful baby mutant calf preserved by the miracle of taxidermy, sans placards, sans glass case, sans roadside museum. A light mass covered in tawny hairs and full of a crumbling, dusty substance, possibly the product of animal becoming vegetable matter. The sweetest bulging brown eyes, which, objectively speaking, are crooked as hell and crusted with glue all the way around, yet they are naive and pleading without being pained. An outlaw, an outcast, qualified to live among the dead. This is my golden calf and I have no qualms. She practically glows. She smells like victory, like heaps of gold coins, salty sweat, and the quickest draw. Champion of bounties. Her presence feels almost too real to bear. All the details I tried to remember are now in front of me, evidence of devotion. I reach back from the passenger seat to pet her; any softness in her coat took off long ago and she feels rough and fragile under my hand. We pass under a streetlight and a glint winks off the gold lid of Bonnie's jar.

*

It takes a few seconds to leave Fort Sumner behind and then the only light comes from our headlights and the dashboard and the moon through clouds; everything else is inky and hidden. I think about spilling the drama of the past few days to Kit, but I want her to spill first. "So tell me—where've you been?" I pick up Bonnie's jar, roll it in my hands. There's notably less in it than before.

"Well," Kit adjusts her grip on the steering wheel, flexes, stalls, "I made it to the church. Me and about a thousand other people—like it was a great pilgrimage weekend or something. I mean, there were busloads of people: in wheelchairs, with walkers, crutches, babies being carried, children—older children being carried like babies. The line stretched out to the highway. I almost turned around."

"It didn't make you want to try selling to them? A captive audience? I thought that was the plan."

"Well, I thought about that, right? Here's all these people willing to seek something out, willing to wait who knows how long just to get a handful of dirt that, at the very least, has been blessed by someone, to do what with? Anoint their ailing parts? Make a holy mud with holy water and smooth it on like a holy poultice? Maybe eat it?"

I realize Kit may feel threatened by the physical object, something that can hit all the ordinary senses rather than just the ultra-sensory ones.

"So for that first day," she continues, "I just checked it out, circled the town, cruised the streets a bit. What's weird is that this miracle church has no advertising. I guess they don't need to. But I didn't see any billboards or bus benches touting magical healing dirt. Almost like whoever's in charge doesn't want to get caught in false advertising or deal with liability? So I slept in the car that night, real close to the parking lot so I could be near first in line in the morning—they clear the line by the end of the day; couldn't tell if the hole had a certain limit it could be dug to or if they just had strict hours. From what I saw, though, people didn't really look any better coming out than they did going in."

"Sounds like it's not the type of place you'd wanna go in an emergency, huh?"

"I don't know—it seems possible that this would be the kind of thing some folks might do first. Why not start with a higher power in an emergency? Why not appeal to a bigger hand than your own? Not saying that's what I would do, but once the idea of a nearby miracle gets opened up, seems like people flock to it as a resource, you know?"

"Instead of what?"

"—?"

"A resource, as opposed to what? What else would a miracle be 'flocked to' as?"

"Are you devil's advocating?"

"No, I just—what are we supposed to do with miracles these days? If you're somebody who believes such a thing could happen—a hole in the ground of a church refills itself each day, or a piñon tree burns and someone believes they're being spoken to by a spirit in the fire, or a holy effigy cries tears of blood—besides going to the thing to witness with your own eyes, what do you do with it except believe it can help you somehow? If it's some conduit for a holy—"

"It's not, though. Let me tell you what happened the next day. When the sun came up, I got in line—still not first, but near the beginning. I stood behind a woman covered in blisters. She could barely stand, but I heard her tell someone it was better than sitting. I thought about getting her the jar of BALMY AIR, but, y'know, didn't want to lose my place and clearly she was focused on the dirt. Anyway. They finally open the doors and we get to go in. The energy is that people are in kind of a hurry but not everyone can move quickly, plus people want to be reverent, so it doesn't move super fast. You file in through the sanctuary and I guess you get some extra prayers in. The walls were pink and it was very... womb-like? People were lighting candles. It was pretty small so they really glowed. On one wall was a painting of some patron saint, a line of lepers waiting to be touched, and the wounds fading from one person's body as hands were laid upon his head. Healed believers in ecstasy, a sort of before and after. Then there was a slope in the floor," she tilts her hand out in front of her, "and the hallway walls were whitewashed and people had hung the things they no longer needed—leg braces, crutches, canes, casts, helmets, contraptions of rubber and plastic and screws—with cards and letters testifying to the effect this miracle had on them. Something to read while you wait your turn, I guess."

"Did you read any?"

"Sure—they more or less said the same thing. 'We tried hundreds of doctors over the years but no one could diagnose or find a cure, hundreds of churches prayed for us and we felt The Spirit lead us here where we were blessed by the dirt and now we can walk and see and breathe again.' Now that I think about it, I don't remember one—not that I read them *all*—saying they went to the miracle site first. It was all 'we were failed by medicine despite our faith which then led us here.'"

She pauses.

"Anyway. It was weird because the temperature in the space had dropped, at that part in the building, but there was also so much body heat radiating off everyone, all of us. The woman in front of me, with the boils, kept letting out these weak little cries, and it looked like a few of her spots were weeping—"

That, too, a miracle of sorts, I think, *that a body would shed tears from places other than the eyes.*

"—So I'm looking at everything on the walls and observing her but not really saying anything to anyone, and then we turn the corner to this little closet-size room and there's the hole, marked out by cords and stakes, something between a safety hazard and velvet ropes. And this woman falls to her knees. One of the nuns—there are nuns sort of posted everywhere, helping people along—one of them kneels down with her and sort of hovers a hand over her back. And the woman, full body trembling, reaches toward the hole—it's like just a few inches deep, maybe a foot or so across—and then the nun reaches, takes the woman's hands, and folds them back toward the woman's body. Only clergy people are allowed to remove dirt from the hole, it turns out, and even then they use a special scoop—nothing ornate but, like, a serious little spade. A nun who'd been standing behind the hole was holding the scoop and she knelt down and dug in. The first nun pulled out a little paper bag for the dirt and the other nun dumped it in with all the ceremony of getting dried beans from the bulk bin. Then I think they said a short prayer with the woman and sent her on her way. Then they looked at me expectantly, so I also knelt down. It was kind of dim in there, just light coming in from a small, high window, and the dirt looked...soft. Fine and dark, velvety soft, no rocks or roots or bugs crawling around. Not like potting soil, though, more natural than that. Almost like coffee grounds? But not...I don't know, there was something inviting about it, something that did make me want to plunge my hands in. After a moment of this contemplation, the scoop nun and the bag nun did their thing, closed their eyes and said some words in Latin, and sent me down the hall to the gift shop to pay for the dirt."

"You *bought* some?"

"It's in the glove compartment."

I open the door and there it is, illuminated in tiny lightbulb glory, a brown paper sack folded around Kit's purchased portion of miracle, next to the baby-food size jar of BEGINNER'S LUCK, on top of the car manual, mini flashlight, paring knife, envelope of car registration and paper-clipped receipts. The bag has the approximate heft of a doughnut. The bag is blank. The dirt smells promising, like minerals.

"How much was it?"

"A few bucks. There was a sign saying the proceeds went to upkeep of the church and feeding the nuns or whatever. They had all sorts of little crucifixes and saint figurines and milagros, too. I was hoping for a bumper sticker saying DIG THE HOLE-Y SPIRIT! but no luck."

I smile and say, "I missed you, sister."

"So then I get outside and the line of people is stretched down the street again. Again, I think about trying to sell something to these folks, but it just seems sort of mean now? Who wants someone like me coming up to them with something that can't cure them when they've got their hearts set on something touted as a miracle? Plus, I'd just had something sold to *me* and it's...it felt weird, being on the receiving end. So anyway, I got kind of turned around in the parking lot trying to find the exit and ended up way around the back of the church—it backs up to some hills and there's these big boulders and piles of salvage wood and a chicken coop. And I see another nun out there, toeing around in the dirt, smoking. I'm pretty sure nuns aren't supposed to smoke, right? So I think maybe she'll also spill the beans about how this all came to be. So I get out of the car and go over and ask her, 'Excuse me, just hoping you might know—why aren't visitors allowed to touch the dirt while it's in the hole?' She takes a drag and looks at me with these eyes that are just steely cold, like, predator bird eyes—"

"Oh, no—"

"It was just her eyes, Gloria, it's fine. So she sizes me up and then kinda smiles and says, 'It's part of the plan.' 'Plan?' I say. And then she gestures to the hills behind her and says, 'Well we can't just have anyone handling this stuff, right?' Then she tells me about how the nuns count how many scoops they dole out each day so they can bring in the right amount of dirt from the hills each night—"

"What!"

"*And* they sift it! Twice! That's how it looks so nice and soft and clean. She said they also don't let visitors touch it because of contaminants and bits of skin that might fall off someone's hands."

"So there's no miracle."

"Well, there's the miracle that they've kept this up for so long."

"Jesus."

"Jesus probably wouldn't be okay with it."

"What if she was lying to you?"

"She showed me the part of the hill they dig from. There was a pick-axe, wheelbarrow, sieve, the whole getup."

We pause.

"I touched *that* dirt. It felt sun-warmed, and then cooler, and I was up to my thumb in it and it felt… like… running water, like a stream in this dry hill. *Just* inside. But I pulled my hand out and it was as dry as it went in. I was going to ask the nun about it but she was walking back toward the church and told me to scram since she wasn't even supposed to be back there. So I went back to the car and just sat there for a while. And it's weird, because ordinarily I'd want to try to get any of that in a jar, and I guess I could've tried for anything that might've been hanging around my hand, but I decided to just let it alone. Like somehow it made more sense—felt more right—to just let it remain a mystery. Maybe there is something miraculous in that hill, in the dirt, the earth. Something that was there before the church."

"Maybe it was you."

"Hmm?"

"Maybe something in you needed to be surprised." Ahead of us, our headlights wash out the color and detail of the landscape we drive through, twin lamps illuminating circles before us, the focus moving forward only, leaving darkness behind. "So then was there some miracle there, in the hill?" I ask.

"I'm not sure what it was. I'm not sure what makes a miracle…or if it's just a class of the supernatural. Does it need to be a spiritual force?

Does it need to incite a change or bring a healing? Because if not, if what I felt in the dirt could be called a miracle," she turns her palms toward herself, forearms braced against steering wheel, "then wouldn't each of our jars contain a miracle, too?"

*

THOUGHTS ON "MIRACLE": colloquially used as a Big Save, the prevention or rescue of what looks to be a lost cause. A stunning feat, not wholly dependent on the medium. That is, from the heavens or from the hands of man. A god's grand gesture. But also something that depends upon the recipient—the more desperate you are, the smaller the gesture can be (economy of scarcity)—it can be a measure of grace or kindness rather than an ark in a flood, for example. Perhaps simply a feeling, as brought on by a jar, that this reality or world is not all there is, that much more exists beyond the five ordinary senses if we can only tap into it or let it emerge from within ourselves.

*

We're driving into deeper night and I'm wondering what's there to just fall out of me, like blood. I picture myself as the sky, high above the earth: full of holes where the stars are, little holes where light falls through, heavier than me and drawn to earth. Here I am huge and not human. This leads me to remembering catching fireflies and other bugs in jars, punching holes in the lid so air might get in. An early instance of capturing, keeping. The bugs always died within a day or two—whether because of no oxygen, no food, or just their lifespan was hard to tell, but all you were left owning was a jar of dead bugs, lights out, rattling around trying to revive them.

I relay this memory to Kit. "What is the difference now? That we can't see them? We don't punch holes in the lids because we don't want them escaping, these things with life that don't need atmosphere." The air in the car is becoming thick with calf must.

"They're specimens," Kit says, "in a way. We are the people who gather them. Share them with other people. Call it redistribution."

"But before us, before this practice—things just flew off, zoomed around in the air, got breathed in and woofed out. Maybe floating up way high because they're less dense or thrown up by wings. No human intervention."

"Where's this coming from, Gloria?"

In the dark, I can say it. "I guess I don't know if I believe in ownership anymore." Kit looks like she might throw a jar at my head if we hadn't been driving.

"Why the hell do you want this damn calf, then?"

She doesn't seem to understand I had freed it. "A liberator is different from an owner, an adopter, isn't it?"

"You just moved it to a bigger case, that's all." Her arms are stuck out straight between her and the steering wheel, pushing her back into the seat. Scab on her elbow like a black island on a map, the edges are that neat.

I think about it for a mile. "At least this one has wheels and an engine," I say.

*

We can't decide on whether or not the dirt was a miracle, or whether or not the calf had needed saving, and this indecision implies that we are not necessarily the authority on such things. Or we don't want to be, can't decide how to be, at this moment.

"I don't know, I need a break from thinking about miracles," Kit says. "What did *you* do, how was the road for *you?*"

I think of both Betty and Rosemary asking me what I was doing on the road. Feel the same where-to-begin agogness.

"Well, first, after a lot of waiting, I hitched a ride with this woman and her dog. They were headed to the Very Large Array—"

"Like for research?"

"To *listen*. She talked about being able to sense things too. I camped with them for most of a night but left and walked in the dark through the next day—"

"No hitching?"

"No. Just walked, no big deal. I thought a lot, a lot about Bonnie." I don't tell her about being robbed or spilling blood. I imagine the shame she might cast on me if she knew it had happened while I was sleeping; maybe I'll tell her later, in the dark of another night. "But eventually got so hungry with no food in sight that I went up to the first house I came across—there was chicory in the yard, and I figured I could at least try to eat that—remember?"

"Oh, yeah. Yuck."

"Well, the lady who lived there, Rosemary, was really kind and generous and let me come in. She fed me, let me clean up and take a nap."

"Really," Kit says, not big on trusting.

"I know you're suspicious, but is that really so different from the hospitality of the Calamity Janes?"

She chews her lip. "I guess not, not really."

"They outnumbered us, too."

"I guess it's just because I wasn't there."

"Well let me tell you where my trusting led me. She had a horse in the backyard. A horse without eyes. A horse who, while it was going blind, bucked Rosemary's daughter off her back and killed her."

"Whoa."

"I know."

"She kept the horse…well, how couldn't you, I guess."

"What do you mean? I was surprised—I figured most people would just see it as a half-ton reminder of a horrible tragedy. It'd be pretty excruciating to live with, I think."

"Well, but it holds so many more good memories of her daughter, right? And with no eyes, it's more dependent, maybe something she can kind of mother, in a way."

I remember the feeling of being cared for as I fell asleep on her couch that morning.

"She did seem like she couldn't help but take care of things that needed it—her garden, that horse, even me."

"So," Kit says, sitting up as if to get out from under some sentimental feeling she didn't expect, "did you fall in love with this eyeless horse, too?"

"A little bit," my sheepish grin. "There was something so entrancing about her face, the absence of her eyes, the way it looked so natural, like she just happened to not have eyes in her sockets. And I felt something invisible."

"Really?" Excitement in her voice.

"Yeah—I think it was the last moment of the horse's vision, while it was running. Luckily, Rosemary had a jar handy so I was able to capture it. And I gave it to her."

"Oh, boy. Did you explain?"

"I tried to? It was hard, with the jar holding something so heavy. But I think she understood. I wish she could have felt what I felt from the invisible, though, that same rush and run, that horseness."

"Maybe she will."

"Maybe." Deep breath. "And then I started walking again, and there was hail, and the road was long and sloping and before I knew it I was back at the museum feeling like I knew exactly what to do. Like the calf was whispering in my ear."

Then we take the next exit, following the signs for late-night food. In search of burrito platters once more, a small feast to celebrate being reunited.

We spend the short night in the car, parked inconspicuously (we hope) in the corner of a mechanic's parking lot. At dawn we drive northeast toward who knows what. The road is empty and feels like it's ours, as if confirming some victory in finally having the calf (my heart pounds) and finding each other again. Or one of us being found by the other. The road always looks the same, the width, the texture, the blackened smears of roadkill, the cracks in the painted lines. No surprises on the pavement itself. Which means it's taken for granted but probably doesn't mind; it's a medium itself, conveying or relaying us between two places and the present (soon past) and the future (soon present, and then passed).

This is the history of roads: first there was land, then there was a way.

*

We get caught under some clouds; it rains, hails again, then shines bright and warm as if it never happened. We roll down the windows a bit and I like that the calf is getting some fresh air, even at the risk of bits of her blowing away. I imagine her puppy-like, happy tongue lolling out of her mouth, head out the window. Whatever it was that connected between her and me when we met feels this joy of life in the air.

*

At a rest stop we pee, feed dollars to vending machines, eat corn chips and a candy bar, and set up shop at a picnic table toward the exit. We haven't sold together since right before we split, and we find ourselves taking jars out to set them on the table rather than just leaving them in the trunk or on a blanket on the ground. I don't remember how many jars we started out with, but the supply has clearly dwindled.

"Where's that one you got from the ghost town?" I ask. "I never saw what it was."

Kit looks over the jars, scanning the labels.

"Ahhh, this one," she says, and holds up LAUGHING WITH GLORIA THROUGH TIME AND SPACE.

"*That's* what it was?" I'm surprised, but what did I expect? To have less of a hand in it, to have been no concern at all?

She looks at the jar in her hand and smiles. "Don't think I wanna sell this one."

Several minutes or a few hours pass, it's hard to tell with the slow traffic and the static sun. The light passing over our jars makes halos of reflected light and shadow ring out from each of them. We shift around from standing, sitting, rearranging jars, for some reason just choosing to bide our time here, like we're shy with each other about trying to make a sale. Eventually we relax on the trunk and back windshield of the Honda, too salted up to move just yet. Breeze washes over us.

"The sun on my skin makes me feel like melting butter. Like I could spread over anything, flow like gold into the bends of my surroundings."

"I feel more like a frying egg," Kit says. "Sizzling, that yolk contained inside the ring of white."

"One thing about that church," she continues, crook of her arm draped over her eyes, "the nuns all, like, live together and cook for each other. There was a doorway between the gift shop and the kitchen of the convent. All that chopping. Kitchen sounds. It looked nice."

I know we're both picturing the meals it took all three of us to prepare, the music of our chopping, stirring, grinding, or the way Bonnie made waitressing look like dancing, body moving deftly behind the counter from line cook to customer, being the moving center of the whole diner.

"That does sound nice," I say. We look at each other for a long beat, then with near-perfect symmetry, we slide off the trunk, pack up our jars, and get inside the car.

Kit drives. The car smells strongly of the calf, which bakes through the window—the sun brings out old books, wet dog, a jar of change, saddles, a barn.

We drive west and after a few miles, I see a white spot on the shoulder in the distance, get a plummeting in my gut. It isn't until we get closer that I know why.

The white El Camino: still covered in dust, surrendered with its hood up, girls clad in broken-in white leaning against the roadside doors, one with a dark buzzcut, the other with red hair still whipping in the wind.

Soon as we pass, Kit says, "We should stop and see if we can help."

My brain stammers. Can't put up much of a fight without telling her what happened. Maybe it'll be fine; maybe it'll be the proverbial carpet pulled out from under me all over again. She looks at me a little strangely, my apprehension. "The all-white thing is a little weird, but maybe they just need a jump," she says. "Glor'?"

My palms get damp, my muscles flush with the memory of adrenaline and I remember how angry I was after my pack had been pulled out from under me. I wonder if she'll recognize me. "Sure," I say, already getting out of the car, "let's see if we can help."

I walk up like this town ain't big enough for the both of us, put my hand on the folded knife in my pocket, not wanting to use it but remembering that I *did*.

Kit gets to them first, of course, asks what they need. The redhead girl speaks low, gestures in nods. I hang back by the exposed engine that just looks like an engine: dark, dusty, greasy, ubiquitous. Peripherally, the other girl—the getaway driver—and I eye each other. I walk around the car as if to check the tires, to admire the ride, but I'm looking in the footwells for anything that might be mine. Nothing. Maybe they dumped it already, spent the bit of cash. They don't even have it to return to me. This car-breakdown is probably a scam too, to take advantage of an innocent traveler's generosity. I make my way around the truck bed—length of rope coiled in one corner, a cinder block in another. I take a deep breath and step closer to Kit. She points to the redhead and says, "Randy was just saying their engine overheated, or maybe they need transmission fluid, aren't sure yet. Do you remember seeing a sign for a gas station recently?"

"No," I say. "Randy, can I see your ankles?"

Two "*whats*" come out of Kit and Randy, the driver girl snorts.

"Your ankles. I want to make sure you're the one I cut after being robbed."

"*Robbed?*" Kit says.

Randy's face goes white, then pink.

"Yeah." I don't take my eyes off Randy. "I didn't want to tell you because I felt ashamed and thought you'd be mad or disappointed, but it seems the road has led me back to the thieves anyway."

Randy lifts her chin and says, "I don't know what you're talking about—I'm not a thief."

"I was asleep. In the daytime. Way off the side of the road—what could you possibly've thought I had that was worth stealing? Did you enjoy the few bucks? The sewing kit? The feeling of my pocketknife cutting through your skin right as you ran away?" I kick a rock, real tough. "I don't know why I thought *I* was the one who should be ashamed."

"Gina, let's go," Randy says to the driver girl. Gina slams the hood down, slides back into the driver's seat and starts the car like nothing was ever wrong with it. Just as Randy turns away from me, Kit ducks down and grabs her around the knees. "Check her ankles while you can, Gloria!"

Thin and bony, pale as sour cream, smudged dirty around the shoe line, mirror images of each other except for a crusty red dash on the outside of her right ankle, arcing over the Achilles. She's yelling and pummeling Kit's head and back with her fists, but Kit doesn't let go. Kit never lets go.

"Well?" Kit says.

"That's mine all right." A bit proud, a bit vindicated, a bit oh hell what comes next. I feel no need for a trial, a conviction. She can't give back what she really took from me. I remember thinking of what Bonnie would do after being robbed like I was, how I imagined her moving on about it. A thin current of anger still curdles along in my veins, but I move to face Randy. Gina leans her head out the window; I imagine this is how she spends her days, poised to do what she's told.

"You can let 'er go, Kit."

Randy's face is knotted into a deep scowl, nostrils flaring, lines on her face are deep and her eyes look like trapped animals.

"You want your money back?" she says. "Here, take it," and flings some change from her pocket. No one moves to pick it up. Some stranger will find it later.

"Would you do it again, if you saw me asleep, backpack under my head like that, unsuspecting and unknown and alone?"

She tries to spit in my face but her mouth is too dry.

"Clearly you're a little curious about my thoughts on this or else you'd be fleeing this scene just like I know you can," I say. "And I think you should. I think you should go home, or make one, find one, call your mom—"

"I think you should mind your own fucking business," she snaps.

"I probably should, and maybe I am. You swiped my business out from under me, remember?"

"What do you want? Do you wanna hit me or something? What?" She jerks her head toward me like a chicken.

I don't know what I want from her. I want it to have never happened. I want her to feel what I felt, but I don't want to cause those feelings. The girl in the museum parking lot rounding the corner to surprise, keeping me in her sights as she walked away from me.

I look her square in the eyes and don't blink. "I want you to think of my face whenever you make the choice to take advantage of someone. My face—which is not terribly unlike yours—appearing in your mind, closer than we are now, even, whenever you make the split-second decision to rob someone or scam someone or push someone around. Think of my face, and be glad I didn't do more damage when I had the chance."

I turn away, grab Kit's hand, and we walk back to the Honda. We sit inside in silence and watch the El Camino pull off the shoulder and drive away, first in the rear-views, then out the windows, then the windshield. Randy's middle finger wags out the passenger window.

Kit starts the car. I sigh and look in the backseat at the calf, which I stole.

*

We drive in silence for several tens of miles. I keep a tally of tumble-weeds. We pass a crudely made sign that was once advertising a store for pornographic videotapes and now just says WILD GIRLS.

"I get why you didn't want to tell me about that," she says.

I scrape the dirt out from under my left fingernails with my right fingernails.

"And I'm sorry it happened to you," she continues. "I don't think you should feel ashamed, and I'm not disappointed in you."

My left fingernails clean under the right ones, hands a little shaky.

"I could never be disappointed in you." She pulls the windshield wiper control toward her, cleaner fluid and bug guts streaking in front of our faces.

"Did you hear yourself talking to her? I mean, damn, Gloria, that was some tough shit!"

I let out a laugh and finally look up at her. "Coulda gone a lot worse, I guess," I say, and take a deep breath in, and let it out.

"She's gonna be, like, haunted by your face in everything she does now."

"Not a bad view," I say, and smile at my sister.

*

We're stopped and I crawl into the backseat, wedge myself in with the calf. She's not exactly stable or comfortable-looking in any orientation, not quite having a flat side, but we put her as much on her back as we could so her legs are mostly up in the air. Kit is outside, jars out in the sun, the old sign—which I notice has faded—pointed toward oncoming traffic.

I cradle the calf's upside-down face, my hands along the sides as I did with the Day-Mare. Her snout, once tender and slick, is hard and peeling at the edges of her fixed nose, along her crudely closed mouth. In the corner of her lips, tiny glue bubbles, the illusion of saliva and breath, of living. Trapped air. The hairs along her nose up between her eyes are

96

traceable, divided left and right and then by brow. Her eyes are dull black glass, at least in this light. I lick my thumb and try to polish them, careful of the few eyelashes she still has attached to the lids, eyelashes long and blonde. I bend my neck and back to turn my head as near upside down as I can, close to looking her in the eyes as I can. The sun hits directly in her right eye of glass, and I angle away from the glare so I can see down into it. The glass has a depth, the blackness has dimension. An angle of facets, perhaps the back of the eye or the place her skull opened and was filled with something—bits of wood, rags, sawdust. Plugged up. Had I done well at memorizing her, between meeting her and now? Or did I add too much fantasy, put her on a weird pedestal of golden hope and wild fascination? If I removed the glass eyes, would there be the same mystery as in the Day-Mare's empty sockets? Would something inside the calf be dislodged and freed, light suddenly pouring from the holes, pure and bright as the naked sun? What was the calf's last sight? The world tumbling around her as she tried to steady herself in a pasture, field of vision a field of clover, the image of the cow mother, teat-bound, animal craving for survival, for safety.

*

INVENTORY OF EXPECTATIONS, NOW THAT WE ARE HERE: climactic achievement, hard-wrought satisfaction, the looming "now what," the other side of desire. Does anyone know what to do with Having? After so much energy pouring into Wanting? How to calibrate to satisfaction? How to love this object and/or what I have projected onto it?

I surprise myself with a feeling that it's time to step away from the dead, the stopped. Time to let go of that which is no longer active.

Perhaps: the calf, the jars (some), Bonnie.

Perhaps: time to chase the living.

The direction the dead set you going.

Still, an affection, a magnetic pull, a relief in getting her beyond those undeserving walls. Instant reverence for this preserved creature. Perhaps that's what it's been all along, this capturing—the preservation business.

I look at the calf, her one body trying to be two, or two bodies trying to be one. A twin life carried inside. Are we two trying to be one? The calf didn't survive it, but we could.

The calf in contrast to the horse: the way one is born compared to the way one becomes. No idea where the calf has been other than alive on a ranch and stuffed within a glass case, but the element of time has not used a gentle hand. Hair rubbed away to cracking hide, hair matted like that of an inconsolable creature, hooves chipped and body stuffed into a nearly rectangular shape, unnatural in the face of her naturally bizarre collection of limbs. Whereas the horse was cared for and glossy, finely muscled and every part in the right place, hair growing in the right directions with blood pumping underneath. Improbable grace on four legs.

*

Two kinds of story: someone goes on a journey or a stranger comes to town. You're either inside or you're outside, subject or objectifying. I feel more like the stranger who's come to town—the town of Betty, the town of Rosemary, the town of the girl behind the counter, the town of the calf. I'm the stranger in the strange land of myself. Strange to be bold like this, to break rules and roles like this, to feel sudden and possessed a bit, watching myself in action from the outside. The factor of solitude. But (or because) I did go on a journey, and that's been the story for so long—two of us journeying, just a little aimless but known to each other, and therefore within the identity of two, spinning along by way of each other's gravitational pull. "Someone goes on a journey" implies that whatever happens along the way will add up to something, lead somewhere, either to more life or the hard stop of death. "Goes" implies choice, agency, movement, motion, forwardness, the stepping away from, a leaving (behind, something). And we did leave, we did choose. We left—we chose. Needed movement away from the place of pain at the cost of leaving the place of most familiarity, our patch of desert where we felt like we were drowning (melodramatic and true). Made the Honda a constant motion, landscape smearing through the window at speeds that reminded us we weren't *there*, and also we weren't *here*—when you're constantly moving, you aren't really anywhere. You stop existing a little bit, in that way; suspension. By continuously being in motion, we had put our lives on hold, or so we thought. Close as we could get, anyway.

I had pictured the feeling of victory lasting longer, forever, that I would have the calf as my own, that I would feel whole or at least more complete, that some mystery would be solved and the rest of my life could be in the daze and wonder of whatever epiphany might happen.

So what happened?

Did I just get caught up in a whim, a weird road hypnosis, a limerence made more powerful by separation and all the fantasy it makes room for?

It was an infatuation, a wonderment at this odd, preserved creature (and she had only been preserved because of her oddity; a many-legged ouroboros); she was already on a pedestal of sorts when I met her. But I believe—with everything in me that drew me back to her—I believe that if we had been driving past a field and there she'd been, off to the side of the herd, somehow standing on four of her legs, feeling the sun on her face and breeze around her skyward limbs, I believe Kit wouldn't have been able to stop me from jumping the fence and scooping her up. Ill-equipped but desperately wanting all the same.

So what does that want mean? The Want that ultimately feels more ripe with possibilities than the Have?

Life is full of holes. They can't all be filled; some voids just have to stay that way.

A stationary pet. Something wild but fixed. Something I could love that wouldn't get away from me. Something I could tend to but without much need. Something that had already died, that I had never known alive.

I suppose I could claim to feel more heroic if I were simply taking back what was originally mine, if there was an element of vengeance or revenge to the venture. If the story went like this: back in 1942, my great-etc-grandmother had a small cattle ranch and one night, under a full bloody moon, her prize heifer bore a calf so surprisingly legged and doubled of body, yet both mother and child survived the horror of this beautiful birth. The calf spent her ultimately short life learning which legs might hold and carry her, tasting sweet grass and warm milk, being doted on and shown off to all who had heard of her, a lucky roadside attraction, the original cash cow of the family. One morning there was stillness in the barn, and then the cattle were lowing. As a testament to the fortune of the farm, my great-etc-grandmother taxidermied the calf herself, doing her best to preserve the coat, the expression of the snout, the orientation of the bouquet of legs. Her skills were amateur at best but her crude stitches bore love, as was the family way. One night, under a dark new moon, someone who'd heard about the mutated calf stole her away with intent to profit, first by charging three times her original come-see fare, then by implicating her in a con wherein she was sold to a handful of museums simultaneously for a bogus sum before somehow it was decided she was legally owned by the smallest of the museums, that one dedicated to a young outlaw bandit boy whose legend was bigger than his actual life, and there the calf waited these many years, until the descendant (me) strolled in and knew who she rightfully, righteously belonged to.

But that isn't the story.

It turns out I'm more on par with the fictional con man or the bandit boy. I imagine the small-town headlines, the small-scale scandal, the trouble I might've left behind me.

*

We stop for the night, side of the road, and I pull the calf from the car, a sort of giving birth with the struggling of the body through an opening. Hairs sputtering through the air. Situate her on the ground and regard her in the flashlight beam. Ground the bottom legs into the earth some so she's stable. Circle her. She is the best thing I have ever seen. Wildness embodied, the best body, the most impossible anatomy and I feel the most conviction that no one is worthy of beholding something so beautiful, so unspeakably and inexplicably perfect and true; I reel at the sight of her. And I'm not worthy of her either. I don't know that I'll ever be able to give her justice on this earth, if I'll never not be hypnotized by her presence and pull, if I'll ever fully feel she belongs to me, with me. So I set her as free as possible, as free as she set me. With a road flare from our emergency bag, I set the calf aflame, Kit looking at me like *I know I can't stop you but are you sure you want to do that?* All sparks and then the calf burns bright against the inky deep darkness, flames lapping out of legs like a wheel of terrible wings—ah!—she's finally presented as the apocalyptic, tremendous angeloid creature she was meant to be, has always been! There she goes, there she goes goes goes—

"It's beautiful," I say.

"And kind of sad."

"Yes. It's beautiful and sad." A feeling inside like an icicle finally dropping, detaching with sudden swiftness. "But it's also just fine."

All of the itchiness of emotions—how many times have I just wanted to climb out of my skin, how many times have I thought about what it would feel like to run this car off the road, how many times have I so desperately wanted nothing more than to nimbly exit the unbearable discomfort of being alive, when the spurs of life dig into my tender sides, when the snare of another pulls a little too snug, when the shadow of a mysterious hand comes over me, when the switch gets flipped to FERAL—will the rest of my life really be like this? This constant fighting with—feeling? Circumstances and obligation? What would be preferred: to be nothing, to be the sun, to be the canyon, to be the river, to be not the twitching muscle in the horse's back but the thunder in the horse's hoof. Something that can both rest and be wild. The thing that aches for isolation and the isolation itself. All paths of least resistance lead to—.

It's funny how two things can feel like the Best Thing. How, when it strikes, this desire (ferocious) to not be needed and to need nothing feels like the Best, but when things with this sister are good, there's nothing better—the moments where we fall in love like that. I never want to be without her, and together we can be the sun. Together, that desire (ferocious) finds a home. Together, there is enough air to fill our lungs, enough space to unravel our bodies, enough water to quench a lifetime of thirst. There is enough and we are enough and we need nothing else. These moments where we suspend in the belief that it can always be so good.

That's how we find ourselves, dancing. A song in the distance, pouring from an unseen car, trailer, house, a song about dancing into death, an ecstasy found in obliterating one's self. I feel the trapped-in feeling shaking out of my marrow and down my nerves, my arms and legs pounding and flailing. The music stops and we continue, find ourselves dancing around the calf's blinding light, and we dance like the flames, I dance until I feel free in my own body, a newfound abandon, feeling my whole family singing in my blood, outlaws, thieves, champions, and saints.

*

At the peak of night, what's left: bits of charred wood, sawdust ash, resiny hooves mangled by heat, two orbs of glass, bubbling and cracked and covered in scorch.

Both of us are freed.

We wake up sitting against the car, slumped against each other. Dawn light, lilac and coral, across the ground. I can tell Kit wakes up by the way her breathing changes. We stay so still for so long as the sky brightens, turning turquoise, as the air warms around us, as the loosest, lightest bits of ash blow away in wisps.

"The earth was formed by the licking of a cow," Kit says, voice quiet.

"What?"

"I remembered Bonnie saying that once, when she was trying to come up with a bedtime story for us when we were little. All the mountains and ridges and valleys formed by cow tongue, like a salt lick."

I make a noise like I wish I could remember. "She deserved all the world's salt."

We watch birds fly in and out of trees in the distance, chasing after bugs and each other, all the drama of their lives.

"I'm ready to stay still," I barely say.

"As in?"

"As in I'm ready to stop. I'm ready to stay." I turn to look at her. "Let's go home."

Kit looks into the horizon, silent.

"Would that feel like defeat?" I ask.

"I was just remembering what that would feel like. To be home."

"It won't feel the same."

"No. It won't feel the same as before, but it won't feel the same as how we left, either. But I want to find a new feeling of home, with you." She pauses, looks at me. "Do you want that, too?"

Feel myself clinging, to her familiarity, to the piece of home that my sister has always been. Even though Bonnie won't be there—no more of her being the heart of the house, moving through it, calming it, no more of her singing, her small rituals, her jars organized just so, no more of her laughter, her scent, her diner uniform hanging spotless on the laundry line, no more of her footsteps on the floor, her tucking her day's tip money into a jar she'd painted black, her calling to us from the bath to ask things like what we thought the weather might've been like centuries ago, if we got to be any constellation what would it be, what did we think happened at the bottoms of lakes?, no more of everything she naturally conjured and made a home with, and no more of the grit that works its way between mothers and daughters—I do want to return. Not to try to recreate it, an impossible task, but to make our own version, a new iteration of home in our new configuration of family, a unit of two, surely surrounded by circles of ancestors silently and invisibly guiding us.

"I want to find home with you, too," I say.

We rise up and stretch our sleep-stiffened bodies. Step closer to the pile of ash-was-calf. Do I want to keep any of it in a jar? Would it be too sacrilegious to scoop some of her ashes into Bonnie's jar? Probably. But I at least consider it. Or should it be buried? To hide the last of the evidence and lay her to rest, hidden finally from gawking eyes?

I leave her there. We get in the car, head toward Silver River.

*

A dream about riding on a burro down a very familiar highway (or maybe all highways are familiar now, or maybe all dream highways ripple with familiarity), sweet tufts of hair between my fingers on its back, no saddle, just a low-to-the-ground straddle around its barrel of a middle, ears slightly swiveling sideways and frontways, I bob along over its shoulders and hips, the atmosphere is flamingo-glazed, honey-dipped, blood-oranged, and this fieriness makes the dashboard, my hands, Kit's face, the early morning look all the bluer when I open my eyes as Kit pulls over.

"You can't take one, but I thought maybe we should visit," she says, turning off the engine.

The coolness of night leaves the ground in faint steam as the sun golds up over it. We're a few feet from a fence—weathered wood posts and dark barbed wire—and a herd of a dozen or so cows are about ten feet beyond it. My heart starts humming. I look at Kit carefully, noting how our similar features must be reflecting each other in this moment—her eyes less mischievous than when she pulled us into the ghost town, but still lit with joy. It occurs to me that after so much time spent parallel while driving, I may be more familiar with her in profile.

"You're risking me falling in love again," a half-joke.

"I know. But also," she moves her hand, palm down, in a slow circle between me and the glove compartment, "I feel it again. That same pull I felt between you and the ghost town cabin."

I rub my eyes, still crusty with sleep, try to sense what she might be feeling, a nerve, a twinge, making sure I don't feel like I'm going to throw up again, and it's so strange and beautiful that I may never know what exactly she's feeling, that it stems from me and I get to witness it.

I give her hand a squeeze while it's in midair and say, "Lemme at 'em."

We get out and approach and it's all heavy breaths from cow lungs, stomps like speech from their huge hooves, rhythmic tearing of grass from ground by their teeth, undulations of their lips and jaws, the slow feeding of their massive bodies.

I silently apologize to them for the invention of barbed wire, its thin delivery of violence.

A few of the herd notice us getting closer, turn, face us head on. It's a bit frightening, this confrontational stance, unsure if they'll charge or go back to grazing.

"They're giants," I whisper.

We stand still, hoping they'll get used to us or forget we're watching them.

"We only ever give the jars to people, huh?" I ask.

"I s'pose that's how it's been, yeah."

"I feel ready to start new. I've been thinking—this isn't from a business standpoint, like sales or whatever—but I think with the stock we've been hauling around…I'm proud of so much of it, of what we've managed to reach and sense and share with people, and I think about what we still have that's invisible and the jar of Bonnie and the calf that was never jarred and what's the rest of our life going to look like, and can we keep carrying our family tradition while moving forward and doing things our way now that we're *it*?"

"What are you thinking?"

"I'm thinking," I gesture at the cows, the trees, "gifts for the living, right here."

I see her face move from fear to delight. "For the living," she says.

We walk back to the Honda and open the trunk, look at what's left of our precious cargo. We start sorting and gathering jars into our arms. We press the cool glass into the warm crooks of our arms; the different volumes clink against each other like they're excited and chattering. Armful by careful armful, we set them in front of the fence. The cows keep grazing. When all the jars are there except the ones we decide to keep for strong sentimental reasons, we sit on the ground, morning damp seeping into our jeans. We pause in the newness of this moment and admire our collection, and we begin. With steady hands, we unscrew the lids from each of the jars, set them on the ground or give them a little jostle to help whatever has been inside get coaxed back out, line them up just inside the fence. We empty out LATE AFTERNOON DREAM, HAWK WATCH, POINT OF AIM, TREE FALL, TINY STAMPEDE, CONVERGENCE OF STREAM AND SAND, CROW SOUL, A LAST BREATH, BELL CHIMES, MARROW TIME, CLOUD FEELING, FIRE FLIGHT, COYOTE

CHOIR, BIG PLUNGE, WHAT CAME OVER THE MOUNTAIN, RATTLESNAKE AIM, TARANTULA ACTION, PLUMB LINE GRAVITY, OPALESCENT CLOUDBURST, BALMY AIR, TURQUOISE BREATHS, BEGINNER'S LUCK, BRONZE AGE, NIGHT GREASE, DEAD LIGHT, EROS/ION, RUMBLE, SOUL OF A JACK RABBIT, NIGHTMARES, MEMORY OF A FOREST UPROOTED, MOUSE JOURNEY THROUGH OWL, TAIL NOTE, UNSEEMLY LOVE, WHAT BURSTS IN SPRING, WHAT THE SNAKE SKIN SHED, THAT WHICH TURNED THE DIRT RED (which left behind a circle of bleached dirt after capturing), COLD STREAMS OF LOGIC, OCEAN ECHO, CHICKEN TALK, CRONE'S BONES, PONY EXPRESSION, BREATH OF MEMORY, SOMETHING THAT SHOULD NOT BE LOST TO HISTORY, and we wait.

I put my hands flat on the ground, feel for some softness in the grit, movement under the surface, movement of tunneling insects and roots toward what can't be seen. All of the cows have turned to face us, step closer to the fence, I'm no longer afraid; they seem purely gentle and curious, magnetized. One cow the color of caramel takes a small step forward at the front of the herd, sniffs, pauses, exults a moo. The air between us and them begins to ripple and shimmer, waves of atmosphere phosphoresce, opalesce, invisible souls and essences captured and contained for so long, now called forth by the song of a living creature.

Occasionally, over the years, we had witnessed contents get out when a jar broke or was opened on accident, which is how Kit knew—*a howl, an escape*. But never in numbers like this, never this chorus of different entities, times, places, instances, happenings, ages. The air seems to braid and weave together, a dance of molecules and channels. The cows let loose their voices, the birds in the surrounding trees sing a cacophony of their own, and Kit and I look at each other as our throats simultaneously open to join in; there are no words, there is just a sound like each of us making our presence known, not out of danger or fear or threat but out of *being*, exuberance at being alive on earth in all its history and future for better or for worse.

The light turns forest-fire orange, a cadmium veil around the shimmering mass of invisibles, which makes a steady vibration that carries its own sound, and then like a distant flock in an evaporating fog, the shimmering and the sound carries itself up and up and up until it's just the sky, which returns to its impenetrable blue, the birds resume their regular call and response, the cows go back to grazing, and Kit and I find ourselves looking at each other in silence and I see us again from up above, climbing in the Honda and returning to the road, winding along the river of asphalt that streams back to Silver River, the road we know better than any other, longer than any other; I see us setting the last of Bonnie's ashes free behind us as we tear down the road—goodbye, goodbye, now you are everywhere, we'll see you on the wind—I see us turning off onto the dirt road driveway, the red rocks and stunted trees, the dirt and the grass, the eternal tire tracks navigating us through the gate, see everything how we left it, see the cluster of open and empty jars now coated in dust, see us slow as we get to our house, get out of the car and stretch and look at each other with nervousness which is excitement, see myself take a breath that is big, that fills my lungs, the outside air that I've known for so long, see myself step over the threshold, into the home where we will live.

ACKNOWLEDGEMENTS

Thank you to Kristine Langley Mahler and the wonderful team and readers at Split/Lip Press for taking a chance on this leggy ball of language (and another round of thanks to Kristine for the meticulous and gritty work of copy editing—grit is, of course, what polishes). Thank you to Kate Finegan for editing with such precision and generosity; creating this world has been all the more clear and true thanks to your curiosity and care. Thank you to David Wojciechowski for creating a cover with the levitating cow leg I didn't know I wanted.

Thank you to Lauren Perez for being in my corner from the moment we met and for being a most patient sounding board; you are my Calamity Janes. Thank you to Chelsea Grimmer for all hooves and paws and poems, for drawing me back to the importance of the line over and over. Thank you to all the writers and artists I have been lucky enough to workshop and commune with over the years this story was forming, in classrooms, living rooms, coffee shops, and bookstores; thank you especially to Amber Keller, Mary Milstead, and Hannah Pass for helping me see the size of this story and what could be done within it. Thank you to Leni Zumas and Charlie D'Ambrosio for showing me how the sentence is an opportunity.

Thank you to Literary Arts in Oregon for the fellowship which allowed me to return to New Mexico and trace my steps. Thank you to Stanley and Rose Mary Crawford (and Tesoro) for having a guest house and garlic farm. Thank you to the Billy the Kid Museum for putting the calf back on display. Thank you to Patti Smith for creating the album *Horses*, which inspired the language and crescendos of Gloria's narration.

Thank you to my parents for all their love and support, and for those earliest road trips to the southwest. Thank you the most to my sister, Kate, for teaching me sisterhood/siblinghood firsthand. I'm so glad to be on this road with you; I love who we are with each other.

*

The events in this book, though fictional, occur in many real locations throughout the state of New Mexico; therefore, they occur on lands rightfully belonging to Native peoples. Those stolen lands belong to the Fort Sill Apache Tribe, Jicarilla Apache Nation, and Mescalero Apache Tribe, the Navajo Nation, and the Pueblos of Acoma, Cochiti, Isleta, Jemez, Laguna, Nambe, Ohkay Owingeh, Picuris, Pojoaque, Sandia, San Felipe, San Ildefonso, Santa Ana, Santa Clara, Santo Domingo, Taos, Tesuque, Zuni and Zia.

*

Occasional use of language from *Horses* by Patti Smith, Alice Walker's "Be Nobody's Darling," and William Blake's "The Tyger" has been paraphrased into the text.

COLLEEN BURNER (they/them) is a graduate of the Kansas City Art Institute (creative writing/painting, 2010) and the MFA writing program at Portland State University (fiction, 2014), and an Oregon Literary Arts Fellowship recipient. Their short fiction has appeared in *Fecund*, *Old Pal*, *Black Candies: Gross and Unlikeable*, *Permafrost*, and *Quaint*. They are a coeditor of *surely magazine*. They live in Portland, Oregon.

NOW AVAILABLE FROM SPLIT/LIP PRESS

For more info about the press and titles,
visit us at www.splitlippress.com

Follow us on Instagram and Twitter: @splitlippress